GREEN & RISDEN

A WALK IN THE dark

a collection of spirit stories

A Walk in the Dark: A Collection of Spirit Stories

© Beverly R. Green & Edward Risden. ALL RIGHTS RESERVED.

Peregrino Press | An Imprint of TitleTown Publishing
De Pere, Wisconsin
www.peregrino.press

Interior design by Euan Monaghan
Cover design by Travis J. Vanden Heuvel
Cover image © Peregrino Press. ALL RIGHTS RESERVED

ISBN (paperback): 978-1-949042-13-9
*This title may also be available in electronic and audiobook formats. Visit www.peregrino.press for
more information.*

PUBLISHER'S CATALOGING-IN-PUBLICATION DATA
Green, Beverly | Risden, Edward
A WALK IN THE DARK/ GREEN & RISDEN
1st edition. DE PERE, WI: Peregrino Press, c2018.

Proudly Printed in the United States of America
10 9 8 7 6 5 4 3 2 1

Prologue

AS SIBLINGS INTERESTED IN LITERATURE AND WRITING, we'd thought for some time about trying to do a project together. The idea took shape as a collection of ghost—or more accurately, *spirit*, or what we have termed *redemptive gothic*—stories. Our title is not meant to indicate a walk with evil. Darkness does not necessarily mandate the presence of evil. It does, however, indicate mystery, or an inability to see all things with perfect clarity. Since both of us prefer stories with ameliorative or helpful spirits rather than infernal or destructive ghosts or demons, we felt as though we'd found the right prompt, something that could work equally well for both of us. Beverly Green's *Companion* novels and E. L. Risden's *The Monster Specialist* both involve some level of spiritual guidance that we consider natural rather than supernatural. That element ties all the stories together. So though they derive from the evolving metaphor of walks in the dark, and those walking may find peril in their way, they walk not purposefully into shadows of evil, but instead with resolve towards realms of light. As Shakespeare's Prospero does for Miranda and Ferdinand in *The Tempest*, we've called on our ghosts not to terrify, but to bring pleasure through mystery.

**We dedicate this volume to our mother,
Patricia Ann Carella Irwin.**

PART I

by Beverly R. Green

1. Going Home...5
2. Resting Place...31
3. Eternal Life...37
4. Battlefield...43
5. A Turnover on Downs...49
6. A Bellaire Ghost Story (*with Brooke Moore*) 57
7. The Thing in the Road..63
8. Tall Tales...79

PART II

by Beverly R. Green and E. L. Risden

9. Our Parents' Gift...87

PART III

by E. L. Risden

10. Marie de France Dreams of Steampunk....................135
11. Only a Joust..179
12. Freawaru's Lament...215
13. Letters from Petrarch..235

A WALK IN THE DARK

Going Home

THE JULY SUN BAKED THE LANDSCAPE HOT AND uncomfortable as a small group assembled in the air-conditioned meeting room of the Harley Baker Real Estate Company. After a two year search, Erica and Jim were finally closing on their first house. It was like a dream come true.

When Erica had accepted Jim's proposal two years earlier, the couple had made a list of the qualities they needed in a house. To be specific, they had made two lists because Erica was a list-maker by nature. One list was the "must haves," and the other list was the "not – necessary

- to – life – but – really - really – would – like – to - haves." They looked at a lot of places, but everything fell short in one way or another.

At some point during the search Erica began to wonder if it was her fault that house after house was wrong. For so long it had been hard to believe that her relationship with Jim would survive. Her childhood memories of angry parents, fighting, name-calling, and running out in the middle of the night all haunted her dreams as well as many of her waking thoughts. She had no desire to end up in a relationship like that. How could she tell? What were the early signs of a toxic relationship? She did not know, so at every convenient excuse she pushed the wedding back another month, another six weeks, another season, because how could they get married if they did not have a house? Jim was patient, and since he did not share her doubts, he was willing to wait.

Then one day in April, Erica was driving home from town and decided to take the scenic route. Normally her life was very hectic. Erica taught fourth grade and worked part-time in the office of a local hotel. She rarely had time for pleasure trips through the country; however, that particular day was beautiful and sunny, she was off both jobs, Jim was at work, and it seemed like a pleasant diversion to explore a road that ran along a quiet creek through the country.

Erica smiled and sang along with the classic rock station playing on the radio. The windows were down and the wind toyed with her dark brown hair. Quite suddenly a house appeared on her left, an old, two-story house surrounded by trees. It had the charm and curb-appeal, but even more important, the large, covered front porch that was on the "must have" list. Incredibly, there was a for sale sign in the front yard. Erica slammed on the brakes and turned around. She drove up to the house slowly one more time just to make sure her eyes were not deceiving her. She stopped in front and jotted down the phone number from the sign and drove home with a sense of destiny. What a find!

Arriving back at her apartment, Erica didn't even waste time getting out of the car before she called the real estate agent's phone number. He told her the house had been built in 1900, was currently empty, and had been for sale for quite some time. They set up an appointment for the next day at five o'clock.

When Jim finished his shift at the hospital, Erica was waiting in the parking lot. "Jim! You won't believe the house I found today! I was driving home down the St. Andrews Road . . . "

"St. Andrews!" Jim interrupted. "What made you go that way?"

"Well, I'm not sure, but I'm glad I did! I think I found our house! Let's drive over there! I'll show you!"

Jim was amused at Erica's enthusiasm, but had learned that about some things it was just better to give in and do what she wanted. "OK. It is pretty out there. No, you drive. You know where we're going." Jim got in the car, leaned across and kissed Erica, and asked, "What's so great about this house?"

Erica blushed. It was not until that moment that she realized she really knew very little about the house at all. "Ummmm, I'm not really sure."

"What's it like?"

"Well, it has a great front porch." Jim looked at her as though she had lost her mind.

"Aaaaaand it's on a nice grassy lot with lots of trees around it. Ummmm, it's a two-story, tan, sort of, and it looks like it has a basement . . ."

"What are they asking?"

"I don't know."

"Is there a garage?"

"I think so."

"Room for a garden?"

"Oh, plenty of room for a garden!" She was relieved to be able to answer at least one question with certainty.

Jim just shook his head. For the next twenty minutes that it took to drive to St. Andrews, Jim chatted on about work. A storm was approaching and it was getting dark when they pulled into the driveway. "Is it OK to get out and look around?" he asked.

"The man at the real estate company said it has been empty for a long time."

Jim couldn't explain it, but the house seemed to be having the same effect on him that it had on his bride-to-be. They walked around and discovered an equally large and comfortable covered back porch. They tried to look in the windows, but most had drawn blinds, and the ones that didn't were too high up. The wind picked up and there was a substantial flash of lightning, followed by a bellow of thunder that seemed to roll through the hollow like an angry threat.

Jim gently pulled Erica away from the back door where she was standing on tip-toe trying to see between the slats of the blinds. "Come on. We can see more tomorrow." As they ran to the car, the rain began. They did not talk as they drove away, and the clamor of the rain drowned out the sound of the radio.

When they got to town, Erica pulled over at the Chinese take-out restaurant, a nervous wreck for trying to see through the deluge. They sat quietly in the restaurant perusing facebook, twitter, and email until the food was ready and the storm deescalated. As they headed back to pick up Jim's car, steam rose from the still hot pavement and eerily wrapped them in pale garlands. Back in the hospital parking lot, Erica returned to the subject of the house.

"So what did you think?"

"Of what?"

"Don't be obtuse," Erica said, not knowing whether to be irritated or amused, "about the house."

"Well, we'll see tomorrow." And that was that.

The following day, school was chaotic, so Erica's time passed quickly. Four o'clock rolled around, and off she went to pick up Jim. He was a little late getting off work, and Erica fidgeted with the radio station, her hair, the mess in her purse, and a smudge on the windshield until she saw Jim come jogging around the corner. He got in and they moved off to their appointment with the realtor, pulling up in front of the house at exactly five o'clock. The real estate agent was already there and met them at the driveway.

"Hi! I'm Tom Cornwall. You must be Erica. We talked on the phone." He shook Erica's hand.

"Yes, Mr. Cornwall. It's good to meet you. This is my fiancé, James Bright." The men shook hands.

"The door is open," Tom said. "Let's take a look." He ushered them up the front steps and into the house.

In spite of the unseasonably warm day, the house was cool inside, and Erica and Jim found it just as cozy and charming on the inside as they had imagined. They walked through downstairs, upstairs, back downstairs and basement checking things off the lists. Two covered porches, a good garden area, three bedrooms, one-and-one-half bathrooms (hmmm, they wanted two full), closet space, a big kitchen with new appliances (but no dishwasher), basement (but the kind of concrete, unfinished basement one would expect in a more-than-one-hundred-year-old house), garage (not attached), everything clean and neat as the proverbial pin.

When they finished looking, Tom explained, "The house belongs to a widow. Her children didn't feel comfortable with her living here alone, so they took her home with them. That was almost a year ago. Rose Sommers and her husband bought this house when they got married, and the family lived here for seventy years. They raised five kids in this house. Mr. Sommers died about ten years ago, and Rose lived here alone until her kids moved her out.

Seems as though she took a fall and they didn't think it was safe for her to live here alone anymore."

"What are they asking?" Jim was curious.

"Sixty thousand."

Erica and Jim glanced at each other. That was half their budget.

Tom continued, "I believe our sellers are very motivated. They say every time they drive by the house, Rose asks when she can come back home, so they want to take that option away, for her own good, of course."

"Of course," Erica responded with a tiny edge of sarcasm.

Tom and Jim continued talking, Jim asking all the guy questions and Tom doing his best to supply answers about the septic tank, wiring, roof, taxes, and other things, but Erica couldn't resist another walk through. When she came back down the stairs, they said good-bye to Tom. He left his card with the instructions to call if he could be of any further service at this house or any other house that was on the market.

Over the next couple of months, Tom continued to show Erica and Jim houses. Most of them were lovely, but none really spoke to them like the St. Andrews house. Then one day Erica got a phone call from Tom.

"I just wanted to let you know that the price has dropped on the house in St. Andrews. They are now asking fifty-thousand."

"Are you kidding me?" Erica almost jumped out of her chair in excitement. Then in doubt she asked, "What's wrong with that house, Tom?"

"Erica, you saw it. It's a great old place. I think they just really want to get it sold."

"Call ya right back!" Click.

Erica attempted to reach Jim, but seldom could he actually answer a call at work. She texted: *St. A dropped to 50 thous.*

A moment later she received a text back: *What's wrong with that house?*

They just want to seel.

sell, she corrected.

Call and offer 48.

We'll make them mad!

Just do it.

OK

Erica called Tom and Tom called the sellers. About two hours later he called back to announce, "You have bought yourself a house!"

Soon after, on a hot July day, Erica and Jim sat in the Harley Baker Real Estate office with a down payment check and dozens of papers to sign.

The owner, Mrs. Rose Sommers, escorted by her daughter, attended the meeting but was too weak to do much more than nod when asked questions, and to sign her name on the final document. That completed, "Miss Rose" herself handed over the keys. In a shaky voice she said, "I lived there seventy years and I was never scared a minute."

Erica's heart went out to the woman. She looked into her eyes and promised her, "We'll take real good care of everything. Please feel free to come back and visit any time."

The next couple of months were a whirlwind. Erica and Jim planned a wedding, got married, moved in, painted, fixed, and decorated. They went to bed each night exhausted, but loving the old place as their own. The sound of the creek was like a lullaby at the end of each day, and as autumn approached, the wind joined in the harmony. The season changed, and the trees responded in brilliant yellow and orange.

Then late one evening, Erica stood at the kitchen sink washing the dishes. A weird thing was happening. She kept hearing a whining sound. It was a very odd sound for plumbing to make, and it concerned her a little, so as soon as Jim got home, she asked him about it. He checked all over the basement and under the sink, but nothing seemed to be amiss. To Erica's irritation, the sound no longer happened for Jim to hear it. "Maybe it was a cat. I saw a big, black cat out in the yard a couple of times."

"I never saw a cat. Besides, it was coming from inside," Erica defended herself.

"I'm sure it's nothing," Jim comforted his wife. "You'll probably never hear it again."

But Erica did hear it again. In reality, what she heard again was much worse. In the middle of the night, she was awakened by an ungodly wail coming from outside the bedroom window. It sounded like a human child lamenting,

"Nooooooooooobodyyyyyyyy.   Nooooooooooobodyyyyyyyy. Nononooooooooooooboooooooooodyyyyyyyyyyyy."

She shook Jim awake. "Jim! Someone outside is saying, 'Nobody!'"

"Whaaa? Hum? Nobody what?"

The sound came again, and that time, Jim sat straight up in bed, hair sticking out in all directions like a cartoon, from sleep, not from fear. He took a flashlight out of the drawer of the nightstand, then quietly stepped over to the window. Pulling back the curtain, he waited for the eerie sound, and when it started again, he turned on the flashlight, aiming the beam in the direction of the sound.

"Humph. There you go," Jim said, as amused as he could be half asleep. Erica peeked out the window. There in the middle of the yard, startled into immobility, was a huge, black cat, eyes glowing like a specter as they reflected the beam of light. Then like a bolt from the shadows came another large cat, tabby, orange, and they both raced off across the road. "She's in heat. They make weird noises when they're in heat," Jim stated. "Back to bed."

Erica noticed the black cat around fairly often after that. She tried to pet her, but the cat would never allow her to get close enough. Erica named her "Ms. Nobody," and began to leave scraps of leftover food out for her. "She'll keep away mice," was her excuse, but in reality, Erica was fond of cats. About six weeks later, Ms. Nobody gave birth to a litter of three kittens under the back porch. After that, strange noises were common with the kittens growing up and the normal noises of an old house creaking and groaning, and only seldom did Erica ever mention it to Jim.

The leaves turned brown and deserted the trees, and darkness came earlier and stayed later. One evening, as Erica stood again at the kitchen sink washing dishes, the whining returned. At first, she dismissed it as the Nobodys out and about and continued her chore. However, it got louder and longer and it did not sound like a cat or any other living thing. The plumbing? That's what she thought the first time she heard it. She nervously finished up and hurried to get things put away and wished Jim would get home when the sound came again, and it was definitely inside the house! Also, she was sure it couldn't be the plumbing—the water wasn't running! A chill ran up her spine and she threw on a jacket and waited for Jim outside.

Jim got home late because he stopped to get a pizza. By the time he arrived, Erica was nearly hysterical. Jim patiently went inside first and checked things out. "Now, Babe," he tried to be gentle, "you're just going to have to calm down about all of this. I checked everything out and there is nothing wrong with the house. Let's go inside. I'll show you."

Jim was beginning to get very concerned about his wife. She was working awfully long hours and maybe it was just beginning to be too much for her. In front of her, he went about the kitchen area looking carefully into everything. He even switched on the furnace once or twice to show her that the sound was not coming from there. There was nothing else to try, so they took their pizza into the living room and were about to begin a DVD—a light, romantic comedy—when from the kitchen came a long, low whine. Jim's eyes got as round as the pizza and Erica jumped up.

"You heard it that time, didn't you?"

"Yes." Jim headed to the kitchen. The whine came again and Jim listened for a moment, his head cocked to one side, then put his hand up to the window. He smiled and walked over to Erica and hugged her tight.

"I'm so sorry. Look. It's the wind whistling through a crack between the window and the frame. I think there's a fast solution, at least for tonight." Jim went to the cabinet and pulled out a roll of silver duct tape. He tore off a strip and placed it over the crack. "There you go! No more whining ghost! I'll be sure to caulk that up this weekend."

"My hero!" Erica beamed. Feeling vindicated, she kissed him long and tenderly. The rest of the pizza and the DVD were forgotten as they headed up to the bedroom.

Winter came, and with it came the hush of the snow-covered world. The kittens were growing into young cats, two gray tabbies and one solid black cat that looked like his mother. Erica didn't see them often, but she continued to put out bowls of food. The greatest evidence that they were still around was the footprints they left in the snow around the property. Sometimes, Jim joked with Erica about her ghosts. When Christmas came, he made reference several times to the "Ghost of Christmas Past," thinking himself very clever. Erica did not find him amusing.

As warmer weather returned, the young cats wandered farther and farther from home in their adventures, and since they were never tame, they one day went off without so much as a farewell to the one who had kept them warm and fed and they did not return. Once in a while, Erica would spot one across the road or in the woods but her role as benefactor was obviously over, and that made her sad. It also took away her explanation for any random noises in the house. In reality, there was not much to explain, and for that, Erica was quite relieved.

April rolled around and brought springtime with it. It was one year since the first time they saw the house. Flowers began to poke out of the ground all over the property, and whenever there was an opportunity, Erica brought them inside and filled another vase. She was arranging a bouquet of daffodils in a crystal vase and the sun had just gone below the horizon one lovely evening when from somewhere there came the sound of a long, low whine. Erica shivered. Then she remembered. Going to the window she reached toward the frame, but before she could investigate, the whine turned into something else. It became a song, an eerie melody, and it was not coming from the window at all, but from the back porch. Slowly and carefully Erica edged up to the back door and opened the blinds just enough to peek out. The music stopped immediately, but the motion sensor light was on.

Jim came home in a bad mood and he really didn't want to hear about it. "Oh, come on now, Erica! There was no one playing music on the back porch! Do you realize how crazy that sounds?"

"But it happened. I'm sure of it!"

"Maybe you just fell asleep on the couch and dreamed about it."

"No! Absolutely not! I was standing in the kitchen when I heard it and I walked to the door and looked out. It was not a dream and it was not my imagination!" she said a bit hysterically.

"There's no reason to yell."

"I'm not yelling," but she did begin to cry. In that moment, Erica decided that no matter how strange things got, she would not tell Jim any more about it.

Erica went to bed early that night without speaking to Jim. About midnight, she got out of bed, walked to the bathroom, and switched on the light. She was looking at her reflection in the mirror when she realized there was someone behind her. As she whirled around, she woke up. It was only a dream. Erica went back to sleep, but at three o'clock she woke again. At first she didn't notice anything except the way her heart was beating faster than normal, the way a heart beats when one has been startled awake out of a deep slumber. It was cold in the room and she decided to go downstairs and turn the thermostat up just a notch. When she got downstairs, Erica again heard the eerie music. It sounded like someone playing a slow waltz on a harmonica. Erica followed the sound to the back door where she could see through the blinds that the motion sensor light on the porch was on again. Over and over the same song played, and she stood, bizarrely entranced, listening . . .

Abruptly the music stopped. Cold hands touched her from behind. Erica jumped, but she knew right away it was Jim. "Babe, c'mon back to bed. I'm sorry."

Erica sighed. "It's OK. I wouldn't believe me either."

"You know, anything can turn that motion sensor light on—an animal, the wind . . ." Jim put his arm around her shoulders and they walked back upstairs. Soon Jim was snoring, but Erica did not sleep the rest of the night.

The next morning as Jim got ready for work, she could hear him humming in the bathroom. Time to let the resentment go. She thought, *I'll go down and make him a nice breakfast.* However, when Erica walked by the bathroom door, she stopped short.

"What is that tune you're humming?"

"Mmmmmm, I don't know," Jim answered through his shaving cream beard, "just something that came to mind. Why?"

"Just never knew you to be a fan of the waltz before." Unbelievably, it was the same tune as the elusive harmonica player had rehearsed over and over the night before.

Erica tried not to appear shaken as Jim whisked her into a waltz down the hallway smearing shaving cream onto her face and spouting joyfully, "What do you mean not a fan of the waltz? Check out my moves!" and began humming again.

Erica laughed in spite of herself and pushed him away. "Go get ready for work, you big lunk! I'll have your breakfast done in a jiff."

The kitchen was quiet and normal. Erica busied herself with bacon, eggs, grits, toast, juice, and coffee. She arranged plates, cup, glass, napkin and fork as though it were a special occasion.

"Something smells really good down here!" Jim said as he came down the steps. "Wow! What did I do to deserve this?" He sat down and immediately began to shovel food into his mouth.

"Guess it's just because I love you or something." Erica walked behind his chair and stroked his hair.

"I guess I love you or something, too." Jim smiled and Erica gave him a quick kiss on top of the head. "What's your day look like today?"

Jim shook his head slowly. "Working a double again. I'll be home around eleven thirty."

"Well, I'll beat you by a couple minutes then. Gonna jump into the shower. Have a good day."

Jim's mouth was full, but he pointed to his cheek close to his mouth. Erica knew the signal, kissed him tenderly on the spot he pointed out, and headed upstairs to get ready for work, as well. In a few moments, she heard the back door close as Jim left for work.

The morning routine continued as usual. The shower was hot and felt good. Erica got out, toweled off, and went to the mirror to brush her teeth. The mirror was steamed over from the shower's vapor. As she reached for a hand towel to wipe it off, from somewhere deep in the walls the pipes began to rattle. The sound got louder and louder and closer and closer. Erica's terror rose with the noise, her eyes fixed on the mirror. Then she realized that something was standing behind her. She couldn't see an image because of the steam on the mirror, but there was definitely a shadow shape in the glass.

"Get out!" she screamed, and putting her hand on a small pair of scissors beside the sink, she whirled around. Nothing was there. It was in that moment that Erica began to wonder if she really was having some kind of hallucinations. Yes, she had been working long hours, and no, she was not sleeping a lot, and well, yes, she did have quite an imagination, but this was too much. Very quickly, Erica dressed and headed to school. Her classroom was a safe place where she could think about this, at least until her students arrived.

From teaching, Erica headed to job two, answering the phone and making reservations at the hotel. It was a busy evening and she didn't have much time to think about the eerie events of the morning. However, she got more and more tense during her drive home. As she pulled into the dark driveway, the thought crossed her mind to just wait outside until Jim got home. As she walked slowly across the yard, Erica noticed a light on the hill beyond the property line that she had not seen before. *Oh well, fools rush in where angels fear to tread.*

She cautiously climbed the hill and discovered that beyond the trees was a small log cabin with the porch light on. An old man sat on the porch with a guitar across his lap. *This might explain a lot!*

"Helloooo!" Erica called out from a distance, not wanting to startle the man.

He stood up and peered into the darkness. "Well hello there, young lady! What are you doing wandering around this time of night?"

"My name is Erica." She approached the steps. "My husband and I live in the house down the hill. I'm sorry to intrude. I just saw the light and didn't realize there was another house up here."

"Well, welcome to ya. My name is George Ross, but most folks around here call me "Pops." I knew someone had bought ol' Bill and Rose's house. It's nice to have neighbors again even though I can't say I've ever seen you there."

"Yes, Sir. We're not home very much."

"Welcome to St. Andrews, Erica!" They shook hands.

"So, you like music then?" Erica asked, indicating the guitar.

"Yeeees. I enjoy playing on the porch in the evenings. Hope I haven't disturbed you."

"I've just heard the harmonica a couple of times. I did wonder where it came from."

"Harmonica?" George was puzzled. "Don't play a harmonica. Ol' Bill used to play the harmonica, though. We had some real good jam sessions on his porch. People would even stop by to listen. Miss Rose would make lemonade and cookies for everybody. He always played 'Anniversary Song.' Said he and Miss Rose danced to that at their wedding."

Headlights appeared from the drive below. "My husband is home. It was nice to meet you Mr. . . . "

"Pops."

"Pops, yes. Have a good night." Erica hurried off, but she turned and looked back when she got to the tree line, half expecting the house and the old man to have disappeared. No, he was still there. He waved to her and turned back toward the door, picked up his guitar and went inside. Then the light went out, but the cabin was still very much there, visible in the moonlight.

Jim was already inside and sorting through the mail when Erica walked in. They kissed and she asked as innocently as possible, "Did you know we have a neighbor up on the hill?"

"Yeah, I think he's called Pops or something like that. I never saw him; just heard of him at the post office. Why?"

"I just met him. He seems very nice."

"Ummm-hmmmm . . . ."

"I saw his light. He was playing his guitar out on his porch when I walked up."

"Really? Well that's it then! Playing music on the porch. And it also explains why nothing happened all winter; he wasn't playing music on the porch in the snow."

"He, uh, doesn't play the harmonica. He said the man who used to live here played the harmonica . . . out on the back porch . . . in the evening . . . "

"Oh Erica, let's not start that again."

"I know, I know . . . I'm just saying what he told me." Then with some sarcasm, "I guess it's easy to mistake guitar music for harmonica music." Jim gave her a sharp look, and that was the end of that for the night. Erica said nothing about the event of the morning, and she and Jim went on to bed and to sleep. About three o'clock, once again, Erica got up. She walked to the bathroom and switched on the light. Déjà vu. As she looked at her reflection in the mirror, she saw a shadow form behind her. She grabbed hold of the same small pair of scissors that had been left on the counter and yelled, "Get out!" She whirled around and found herself looking into the face of a very confused and sad looking old man. Erica woke up, heart pounding. Another dream. She cried herself back to sleep.

The alarm clock rang early, but Erica got up and got ready at the same time as Jim and left at the same time he did. She did not want to be alone in the house. That moment was coming soon enough though. It was Tuesday and she was not scheduled at the hotel, and Jim was working until eleven again.

During her lunch break, Erica thought over the conversation with Pops. Going to her computer, she went to Youtube and typed in "Anniversary Song." There it was. She hit the key to trigger the song to play. Sure enough, although the music was played on the piano and strings and included the vocals, it was the very same song she had heard on her back porch played on the phantom harmonica.

During story time with her class, Erica sat in her chair in front to read from a favorite book. Exhausted as she was, her eyelids began to droop, and her reading got slower and slower . . . . A small hand touched hers. "Do you want me to read for you, Mrs. Bright?" It was Jason, a particularly precocious boy in the class. "You can go put your head down on the desk if you want." That should have been funny. It wasn't. Erica just thanked him and forced herself to continue, fighting through her fatigue for the rest of the day.

Arriving home on the beautiful, sunny, spring afternoon, Erica felt somewhat refreshed. She found nothing intimidating about the house. Maybe it was all just coincidence, lack of sleep, and a wild imagination. After walking around the house and admiring the red-orange poppies, brilliant in full sunlight, the crimson crabapple blossoms on the trees behind the garden, the plump pink and white peony buds ready to burst open, the bright yellow forsythia, and the hyacinths and tulips that seemed to have bloomed overnight, Erica felt again her original love for the old house and its surroundings. *Yes, I suppose if you're really tired, a guitar could sound like a harmonica.* She went inside and opened the windows and put a small roast in the crock pot. Jim could have a hot roast beef sandwich when he got home, and they could use the rest for lunches for the next couple of days. Then she got a glass of iced tea and her stack of papers that needed to be graded and curled up on the couch. After a bit she dozed off, and when she woke up, it was twilight. With a start, Erica raced over to the lamp and turned it on.

Erica sat back down on the couch and began to grade once again. The house was silent. Suddenly, from the back porch there began, clear as a bell, the sound of the "Anniversary Song" played on the harmonica. Frozen in place, Erica listened to the tune that had become familiar to her. Then a movement from the stairway snatched Erica's attention. A shadow was moving down the stairs. She watched transfixed as the shadow became the figure of an elderly woman bearing a strong resemblance to Miss Rose. The woman descended the stairs to the dining room. She was wearing a flowered dress. The woman did not look at Erica, but walked through the room toward the kitchen. Erica heard the sound of the back door, and in a moment, the music stopped. There was no feeling of threat, no hostility, no unnatural chill in the air. The woman passed through as though she were peacefully passing through her own home.

Erica was still on the couch when Jim came in. "Please, listen to me, Jim. This is all really happening or I'm losing my mind." Jim listened as Erica told him everything. He did not comment. He just held her for a very long time, worry on his face. That night, it was Jim who could not sleep. In the morning, they parted company with a kiss in the driveway, but Jim wished they were spending the day together if only so he could keep an eye on his distraught wife.

That afternoon at the hotel, Erica got a call from Jim. "Babe, I only have a minute. Do you have a newspaper?"

"There's one on the table in the lobby. Why?"

"Go get it and turn to page twelve. I don't think you're going to have any more trouble with your ghosts. Check it out. I have to go. I love you!"

"I love you, too." What in the world did that mean? Erica walked out into the lobby and picked up the newspaper and turned to page twelve. The obituaries. In column two she read:

Rose Barkley Sommers 92— Rose Sommers of St. Andrews died on Tuesday, April 28 at her daughter's home in Crawford. The death was attributed to natural causes. Rose was a former employee of Madison City Water Works. She served for seven years on the St. Andrews Community Board and Volunteer Board. She was a member of St. Bartholomew's Catholic Church where she sang in the choir and served as chairman of the benevolence committee. Rose was preceded in death by her husband William, and a brother John of New Hamilton. She is survived by five children, Mark (Sonia), Luke (Joan), Veronica (Ron) Jenkins, Anne (Henry) Harper, and Joshua (Frances), twelve grandchildren and seven great-grandchildren. Friends and family will be received at Baldwin's Funeral

Home on Johnson Ave. in Crawford on Thurs., April 30 from 2:00-4:00 and from 6:00-8:00. Mass will be held at St. Bartholomew's on Friday, May 1 at 2:00 with Fr. John Stewart officiating. A grave side service will follow in St. Bartholomew's Cemetery.

So it was Miss Rose in the house last night, and her patient, loving Bill waiting for her and playing their favorite music on the porch! And that call meant that Jim believed her! Erica sighed deeply and her eyes teared up. When she had another free moment, Erica went to the computer and looked up quotes From William Penn. There was something she remembered the priest quoting in her wedding ceremony:

They that love beyond the world, cannot be separated by it. Death cannot kill what never dies, nor can spirits ever be divided that love and live in the same Divine Principle; the root and record of their friendship.

The quote continued, "If absence be not death, neither is theirs. Death is but crossing the world, as friends do the seas; they live in one another still." Whether or not she believed it on the day of her wedding, Erica believed it from that day on.

At Erica's request, they went to the visitation in Crawford. Friends and family received them kindly and asked if they were enjoying the house. Erica and Jim both said they were and mentioned nothing about the strange occurrences there. They walked up to the opened casket together and Erica recognized the face of the woman as she lay peacefully in her flowered dress. She gently touched the pink satin casket lining next to where the old woman's hands were clasping a jeweled rosary. Jim held Erica's other hand.

"Thank you, Miss Rose," Erica whispered. "We'll take real good care of everything. Feel free to come back and visit any time."

There was, of course, no answer. Rose and Bill Sommers were never seen nor heard from again on this earth and the sound of Bill's harmonica finally ceased, but Erica grew to cherish the memory of a man's love that was so faithful that he waited more than ten years to accompany his bride to the Pearly Gates, and to enter in dancing with her to the tune of the "Anniversary Song."

A WALK IN THE DARK

RESTING PLACE

(appeared in Emanations: I Am Not a Number,
International Authors, 2017)

IT HAS ALWAYS BEEN A SPECIAL PLEASURE OF MINE TO take long evening walks. The exercise and fresh air ease the stress of the work that often takes me away from home in search of nuggets of history to use in my writing. Exploring new places takes my mind off deadlines and writer's block. I was taking such a walk in a small town in Ohio one evening near sunset when I spotted a walnut grove surrounded by a wrought iron fence. The warm summer breeze seemed to whisper an invitation to enter. The gate was open.

Above the ancient walnut trees a pink and blue patchwork sky spread to the horizon. An antique, war-worn cannon stood just inside the gate, a sentry guarding against time that sought to profane this sacred place. A brass plaque at its base was inscribed with the words:

Dedicated to the valiant men who served in the Union and Confederate Armies and gave their lives for the principles they believed in.

Beyond the cannon, aged granite tablets, some chiseled nearly away by years of weather, held the secrets of the brave individuals who rested there in grace. I knelt beside a fragrant lilac shrub that for years had protected one inscription. It looked as though a blossom had recently been picked, and I wondered if I was alone. Pushing back the branches, I read:

JOSIAH BURNS
PRIVATE
Co. C 7th OHIO

Nearby, a small fence separated a family plot. Bushes that bore the springtime memories of pink peonies drooped between the stones. I entered quietly, startling a squirrel who scurried up a walnut tree chattering, perturbed. Crickets began to intone a lullaby to the souls cradled in the earth.

Ebenezar farmer
Servant of Christ
Who died in his 66ᵗʰ year
January 20 1888
In death as in life
An honest man

Mary farmer
Faithful helpmeet
Died June 16 1865

And a little apart . . .

Elizabeth Farmer
Who left this world
In her seventeenth year
July 2 1863
As in all things
Jesus have Mercy

As I knelt over the grave of 17-year-old Elizabeth considering the many causes that could have brought a young girl to her death in 1863 and why this stone was curiously separated from the others, the wind picked up and chilled. The leaves rustled, and the hair stood up on the back of my neck. Slowly looking up, I saw a young woman standing near the soldier's grave with the lilacs. She was draped to her ankles in a gown of gray linen. Her features reminded me of the carved ivory cameo my great-grandmother wore—delicate, beautiful and pale. She clasped to her breast one of the lacy, purple blossoms. As she approached me slowly, I was transfixed. Her eyes, her dark and sorrowful eyes, touched me. She did not speak, but I saw the source of her pain—the tiny unmarked grave within the grave, the little life that had passed away mourned by no other mortal, because he was unknown to all but her.

> *Have pity on me, O ye my friends;*
> *For the hand of God hath touched me.*
> *Why do ye persecute me as God,*
> *and are not satisfied with my flesh?*
> *Oh that my words were now written!*
> *Oh that they were printed in a book!*
> *That they were graven with an iron pen*
> *and lead in the rock forever!*
> *For I know that my redeemer liveth,*
> *and that he shall stand at the latter day*
> *upon the earth:*
> *And though after my skin*
> *worms destroy this body,*
> *yet in my flesh shall I see God.*

I did not realize I wept until I tasted the salty tears that streamed across my lips. I wiped my eyes, and when I looked up, she was gone, but I knew that by my tears she had been comforted. I also knew what I would write.

A white blaze drew my attention: the light that illuminated the cannon by night. It was nearly dark. I hurried to the gate. Stepping into the street I felt bitter-sweet resurrection. In the breeze I caught the scent of lilacs.

I went back the next morning and placed two yellow roses on the grave of Elizabeth Farmer. Sleep well, Elizabeth, sleep well.

A WALK IN THE DARK

Eternal Life

I THINK THERE'S A TABLE OVER HERE. PLEASE, SIT, AND we shall continue our conversation. You asked if I believe in eternal life. My friend, that is a question that many young people fail to ask of themselves. At your age, it's easy to feel invincible, even immortal, as I once did. I can tell you without reservation, yes, I definitely believe in eternal life, and it was a night just like this, with a perfectly clear sky and a chill in the air, and a moon that was just as full and bright and stunning, that I attained that knowledge. We don't know each other well, but if you'll let me buy you a cup of coffee, I'll tell you how I came to believe in, yes, to understand, eternal life:

My *lesson*, I shall call it, began in Atlanta airport on Tuesday, March 9, 1982. I was on my way home from a conference where I had delivered the presentation of a life-time. Months had gone into its preparation and I had nailed it down to the very smallest detail. Everyone from the CEO on down through the ranks was impressed that such a young woman could accomplish so much, and I thought it was my ticket to a large, comfortable office and a title of my own. My flight back to Pittsburgh was scheduled to leave at twenty minutes after midnight from Gate B36. Anticipating a crowd, I arrived a little early. The baggage check was slow but not unreasonable. I knew I would have a wait, but it had been a long, hard day and I was looking forward to some down time with a cup of coffee and a book. I even thought that I might take a nap during the flight.

The problem was, I couldn't find my gate. Oddly, the further I walked, the fewer people I saw. Slow night in Atlanta airport?—that's an oxymoron. It seemed as though I walked for miles through Concourse B, and then the gate numbers just ended at 35. I shrugged and looked around. The snack and coffee shops that were usually open all night, or so I thought, seemed to be closing. Finding help was going to be difficult with no one around, so I retraced my steps.

Presently, I became aware of the sound of panting, not heavy breathing, but panting. I whirled around and faced an empty corridor. Then I noticed a maintenance man in a blue jumpsuit with a whisk broom and dust pan bending over a corner. He was heavy-set and quite the hairiest man I had ever seen. I walked over to him and asked him for directions to B36, admitting that I was lost. Hearing my own words made me feel uneasy. It was probably not smart to give that kind of information to a stranger regardless of the fact that he was an employee of the airport and probably accustomed to answering questions. Quelling my misgivings, the maintenance man straightened, offered a rather tight-lipped smile, and pointed back in the direction from which I had come. His voice was astonishingly soft if a bit gravelly as he answered, "When this corridor dead ends, turn left, then go all the way to the end of the hall."

Smiling back, relieved, I thanked the man and set out again, thinking that I must be more tired than I thought. Once more reaching the end of the corridor, I saw, sure enough, there was a narrow hallway leading to the left. Just before I turned into that hallway, something on the very edge of my peripheral vision got my attention. For a split second, it seemed like something was there and I could have sworn it was a German Shephard. Slightly amused, I considered *crazy how an over-tired mind can play tricks.*

Around the corner and at the end of the hallway, a room opened up, and there was Gate B36 just as the maintenance man had said. Sighing, my distress assuaged for the moment, I surveyed the scene. A couple of disinterested-looking individuals sat at opposite ends of the waiting area. One man was reading a newspaper and the other was sipping on a drink and gazing out the window at the full moon rising over the roof of the terminal. *Quiet and peaceful, indeed.* I collapsed onto a seat and rifled through my carry-on to find my book and through my purse to find my glasses.

I had heard of "black dogs"—illusions that truckers experience on the road at night. They think they see a black dog running across the road because of the shadow play in the headlights. It usually means it's time for the trucker to pull over and get some sleep. Weirdly, I seemed to be experiencing something of the same phenomenon. Paws and tails kept appearing at the edge of my line of vision, but when I looked, of course, nothing was there.

At some point during the wait, I dozed off. One of those uncomfortable dreams where you're trying to run away from something but just can't seem to get anywhere wrapped around my weary mind. I could hear the old pastor from my grandmother's church that I visited on occasions when I was little shouting as he pounded the lectern, "What will ye do in the day of visitation, and in the desolation which shall come from afar? To whom will ye flee for help? And where will ye leave your glory?" There was a howl from behind me, or was it from in front? It got louder and closer, and then morphed into the announcement to board the flight. I awoke with a start. Trying to shake off the dream, I jumped up too fast and knocked my opened purse onto the floor, spilling half its contents. I knelt and tried to quickly collect everything. When I stood back up, I noticed that only one more person had joined the group: an older woman in a business suit carrying a briefcase. Likely she was someone else like me, a woman who worked too hard and saved money wherever possible, like taking flights in the middle of the night. It just seemed so odd that this flight was not cancelled with only four passengers ready to board. I tried not to dwell on it. I just wanted to get home.

The man who announced boarding was unpleasant and said nothing to us as we presented our tickets and filed onto the plane. I don't believe he even looked up. There were two flight attendants who were more cordial than the man who checked our tickets. One nodded and turned away, but the other smiled slightly and welcomed us aboard. Her amber-gold eyes were a bit unnerving. I found my seat which was by the window, and after stowing my carry-on in the compartment above it, I buckled in and glanced out the window at that incredible moon. The man who had been reading the newspaper sat down beside me and looked straight ahead. Fine with me. I wasn't in the mood for conversation. The other man and the woman with the brief case were directly behind me. For some reason, the maintenance man had also boarded the plane! Why?

The flight attendant with the unusual eyes explained safety procedures in case of an emergency—I didn't pay attention. I was trying to quell a panic attack by rubbing the soft fabric of my jacket between my fingers and counting. The pilot's voice came across the intercom, much like a growl, "Welcome to flight 342, 12:20 red eye to Pittsburgh. The sky is clear and we have been OK'd for take-off. Arrival time should be approximately 1:45. Enjoy the flight and the full moon. " We began to taxi. Soon we would be in the air with no way of escape. *One, two, three, four,* I counted in my mind, but couldn't stay focused. . . *How huge the moon looks from here . . . our Father who art in heaven . . . our Father who art in heaven . . . our Father who art in heaven . . . now I lay me down to sleep . . . the moon looks huge from here . . .*

No one spoke. The plane was in the air. As usual, the flight attendants began making their way down the isle of the plane with the cart of drinks and snacks. The first turned and grinned and I saw her teeth! Her teeth were like the teeth of a canine! The second asked, "Anyone ready for a snack?" All eyes turned toward me—all their amber-gold, up-slanted eyes turned toward me . . .

I did not die that night, but I was *changed*. You see, my young friend, we are all endowed with eternal life which we will spend in one form or another. If we fail to pursue Heaven, Hell will pursue us. Shall we agree with Mr. Milton, that "the mind is its own place, and in itself can make a Heaven of Hell, a Hell of Heaven. What matter where, if I be still the same?" Indeed, *if* I be still the same.

Ah, I believe they are getting ready to close here. Shall I walk you to your car?

Battlefield

MIDNIGHT. MARTIN STANDS AT HIS POST, ALERT AND fidgeting. So far, everything is quiet, but to relax is out of the question. To doze, to drift, to lose focus, could be fatal to more than just himself. The minutes strain by. A jazz number begins to play in his mind and he silently moves his foot in time with the cool, blue, syncopated tune.

Is that the sound of a breath? Martin holds his. Then a creak of the stair, slight—perhaps it is just the house settling. There is nothing more. Martin allows his strained muscles to ease a tiny bit. Not now, but soon . . .

How had he come to this moment? Long ago, eons it seemed, Martin had felt the urge, the *call*, to become a warrior for the defense of the weak and the innocent and, perhaps, in his deepest heart, for the glory, as well. The crisp uniforms, the multi-colored accolades, the shining weapons, and the proud demeanor of the warriors was attractive to him, but it was the challenge, even the discipline, that drew him in. Martin was never satisfied with things made easy, and the training was not easy, nor was it pretty. Seldom was there time to wear his pure white uniform with its gold buttons, to bask in the peace and quiet, or to relax to the sound of gentle music. More often, there was rain, cold, mud, and a sodden field uniform worn for days on end. Sometimes it was the opposite—dry, oppressive heat that did not give in at night, wind that drove the sand into his eyes and nose, and sweat that soaked his socks and collar and hair. Other times there was snow that seemed to slow everything down to the point of negating every strategy. Sometimes the training simulations were so loud that he had to force himself to think, while at other times, the silence was nearly tangible. Always the warriors were pushed to overcome, overcome, overcome.

Weaponry, of course, was part of the training, and weapons were fascinating to Martin. Every blade, every spear, every projectile, was an extension of self, and when properly employed, could save lives. *The weapons of our warfare are not carnal, but mighty through God to the pulling down of strongholds.*

To stay strong and fit was essential. Martin liked to run. No matter where he was assigned, he ran, glad to learn the terrain, the wildlife, and the ways of the people he passed along the way. He had been assigned to many places and had witnessed much—tawny lions in Kenya, glistening sun on the snow in the Alps, mud hairstyles of the Namibians, crystal blue waters of the Mediterranean, seemingly impossible rock formations of the American West, fuzzy marsupials "down under"—the entire planet enthralled him!

With his comrades, Martin had moved from training manoeuvers into real combat. They fought side-by-side against their common enemy, often for long periods, whole countries at stake, always striving until the powers above said, "It is finished." Some had fallen, some were reassigned, and some labored on. The pressure of constant danger was secondary to the great responsibility they carried—the defense of those who could not defend themselves against enemies they did not even perceive. To lose was inconceivable; to lose was not an option.

Because of his stealth and expertise in hand-to-hand combat, Martin began to receive assignments that involved working alone. If an enemy plot against an individual was uncovered, Martin stepped in as guardian angel, a tedious job at times, but one that could provide great rewards— laurels to one day cast before the King.

Now, somewhere on the very edge of his awareness, Martin feels the approach of his enemy. There is no sound, but a slight change in the air. He flexes his fingers several times before they lace confidently around his weapon. The grandfather clock in the hall clicks loudly and strikes one.

A sudden swish, and Martin is grabbed from behind. Graceful as a dancer, Martin spins away as his opponent's blade catches in the fabric of his uniform. No real harm done. Martin is looking into the ruby-red eyes of his enemy. He is close enough to smell the breath like rotting flesh in the fiend's startled exhale. Now face-to-face, the combat begins.

Stepping carefully with blades in hand, the two seem to circle an invisible object, each waiting for the other to advance. Seconds seem like hours, and the sweat begins to bead on Martin's forehead. Like a snake, the enemy strikes out. Martin blocks the strike with his left forearm, returning it from underneath with his right hand that holds the blade. Something is pierced—is it body or just clothing? The assassin mutters profanity and jumps back.

The air is suddenly stifling. A thick, dark cloud seems to be wrapping itself around the two fighters as the one with the sanguine eyes chants an unholy curse in a voice that curdles the blood. Martin knows this will not be an easy victory. His enemy's commitment is no less than his own. *Praise be to the Lord, my Rock, who trains my hands for war, my fingers for battle.*

Those fiery eyes perforate the smoke. Martin lashes out in their direction once, twice, three times, causing the retreat of his adversary into a corner, but awarding no contact. Launching from the corner walls, the demon raises his blade and comes down hard, penetrating Martin's shoulder. Martin dodges down and to the right. He is wounded—not fatally—and he lunges in from behind and buries his blade into the enemy's sinewy back. A scalding howl rises from the foe, but he is not finished yet, and as he pulls away, the blade remains embedded in his muscle. Turning on Martin, it is not only his red-hot eyes that slash the darkness, but his crimson mouth, teeth sharp as razors. In fury, he hurls himself at Martin, but the skilled warrior throws himself aside, and the dark adversary hits the wall breaking his blade. *He trains my hands for battle; my arms can bend a bow of bronze.* The clock strikes half past.

Martin retrieves a second, smaller knife from his boot. In the millisecond as he rises, the fiend dives forward, planting his teeth in Martin's hand—the hand holding the knife. Instinctively, Martin slams a quick left fist square into his nose. The bite is released. The knife clatters to the floor. The enemy is paralyzed by pain. The warrior presses his advantage. Ears ringing and eyes burning from smoke, Martin delivers an upper cut to the jaw and the demon falls, the blade still in his back. Looming above him, Martin pounds a foot into his chest. Turning his head, the enemy spies the knife where it rests on the floor. In desperation, he grabs for it without success. Martin kicks it out of reach. The evil one grabs his other leg, and Martin falls.

Everything now seems as though it is moving in slow motion. Every breath from each fighter is a desperate gasp. They wrestle; they roll; they writhe. They know the end is near for one or the other. Martin forces his adversary onto his belly, jerking his arm up behind. The demon struggles. Martin's last strength is spent in this hold. *I overcome by the Blood of the Lamb!* The accursed enemy makes one more desperate attempt to pull out of his bondage. There is a crack like a splintering of bone, and a howl that shakes the gates of the nether world as they receive the villain and slam shut. The clock strikes two.

The smoke rolls quickly away and the stench of battle is replaced by calm, fresh, night air. Silvery moonlight swathes the room in a hallowed peace, and Martin the Guardian turns his green eyes heavenward as he salutes the King and then returns to his post.

✷ ✷ ✷

Meanwhile, Alexander sleeps peacefully in his crib, sky-blue eyes gently closed, lashes fluttering only slightly, a sock monkey clutched in his tiny hand. He is blissfully unaware that there is war in the heavenlies, and that a battle has just been fought for him.

A Turnover on Downs

I WILL NEVER FORGET THAT DAY! HOMECOMING IN Tuscaloosa is always big, I've heard. But then, any football game in Tuscaloosa is big—larger than life, you might say.

Alabama Homecoming 1993 began with a huge influx of fans arriving for the game. Finding a parking place was a challenge, even at the early hour. We moved through town at a snail's pace, decided on a lot that looked "good," paid the man who waved us in, and were directed to a parking spot in the nearly packed back yard of a rather run-down house. The cars were squeezed in so tightly that I actually sucked in my breath to be able to exit the car. The spot was close enough to the stadium though, so I was happy. Even the children were excited and raced a little ahead.

"Angela! Ryan!" my wife Janet called them back, sounding tense.

"I've got 'em!" My best friend Joe sprinted ahead until he caught up with the children. Younger and with no children of their own, Joe and April were like a second set of parents, cooler and less-stressed than Janet and me.

With Joe in charge of the children, Janet settled into a casual walk beside April as they discussed plans for the rest of the weekend. We had reserved our motel rooms for the whole weekend so we could feel like we were on vacation one last time before the autumn chill arrived.

I walked behind the others, left alone with my thoughts and observations.

We stopped to visit the Paul "Bear" Bryant Museum and strolled through the Hall of Honor, chuckled at the "old-timey" uniforms on display, perused the photographs and paintings, and exclaimed over the Waterford crystal replica of Coach Bryant's Houndstooth hat. Bear Bryant—what a coach! I remembered a quote from the Coach that had always inspired me: "If you believe in yourself and have dedication and pride—and never quit, you'll be a winner." Did I believe in myself? I used to think so. Then Daddy passed away and I was no longer so sure.

We moved on to the quad which became busier and noisier as vendors opened their booths, radio stations wired for broadcasts, and Crimson Tide celebrities of past and present paraded by, striking an almost religious awe among the onlookers. Music from marching bands, rock bands, and country bands mingled with the sounds of early cheers and greetings from friends. Young people, old people, and every age in between dressed in jeans, shorts, or formal attire, ate, drank, sang, danced, shopped and chattered under the watchful eyes of mounted policemen. My heart beat just a little faster than usual in anticipation of the event to come. It was a perfect afternoon.

As kick-off time approached, we joined the crowd moving toward the massive, newly-renovated stadium. Entering Bryant-Denny Stadium, as always, was a thrill. Coming in from the bright sunlit street, the cool of the concrete cathedral was a relief. I checked the sections and numbers on our tickets and led my little band a short distance through the halls, dodging fans waving pennants and carrying beers. As we stepped back into the sunlight on the other side, the field spread before us, brilliant green and alive with crimson and white! Color and sound were everywhere and I was swept quickly into the passion of the event!

The game began in a burst of energy, and eventually developed into a real cliff-hanger, but the Tide came through at the last moment with a field goal making the score 20-17, a coincidental tribute to returning hero Van Tiffin who had pulled off the same trick in '85 against Auburn. The close games were always hard on me. I should have been elated at the victory and charged for celebration, but as we wove our way out through the crowd a strange melancholy settled over my mind. Finally, I tossed the car keys to Joe, and sent my family and friends on to eat ribs at Dreamland, promising to catch up to them later at the motel.

"You OK, Honey?" my wife asked, a little concerned.

"I'm fine," I answered, and pulled her close and kissed her on the top of her head. The smell of her shampoo lingered in her hair which was just a bit damp from perspiring under the sun all day. "I'll catch up to you before bedtime." So they left me, maybe a tad reluctantly, and went off to dinner.

University Boulevard, which a few hours earlier had teemed and seethed with a flood of hot and happy fans, now cooled and quieted in the soft October dusk. The smells of smoky barbeque and blackened steak still hung in the air, although the vendors were gone. Finding myself in front of Denny Chimes, I decided to take one last look at the Walk of Fame. The old oak trees rustled as though baffled and searching for a remnant of the brouhaha that had recently passed under their boughs. Silently, I read the names on the walk: Pat Trammel, Johnny Musso, Joe Namath, Major Ogilvie—all the greats once stood here. The Tide's tradition of victories is unmatched anywhere. I found the square marked "Jay Barker" and sat beside it on the steps. Nineteen-ninety-two—what a season!

For the hundredth time that day I thought about my dad. Daddy would have loved today. He was a real Alabama fan, all the way to the bone. It was hard to believe that he never made it to Tuscaloosa for a football game. Always at home, the games had blared on the radio or the television. We cheered the victories together, cussed when things went wrong, and even cried a time or two when defeats were especially painful. Daddy was still pulling for his team when his body succumbed to the emphysema that had haunted him for years.

Yes, Daddy would have loved today. He would have been here, too. I would have insisted. My thoughts made me realize the reason for my mood. I always missed my dad, but I missed him most on days like this. We should have done this together. We should never have missed the opportunity.

The street lamps came on. I sighed, more loudly than I realized. It caught the attention of an old gentleman who was strolling by. He walked over and sat beside me on the steps, removed his hat and set it gently down beside him. "Good game this afternoon. A few bad moments, but a victory is a victory."

Yes, Sir," I answered. I really didn't feel like talking.

"So why are you so low, Son?"

I looked at his face for the first time. He was like one of those oak trees over our heads—old, but strong, what one might call rugged. That's the kind of voice he had, too. His eyes held that rare wisdom that comes from carrying the responsibility of years of decision-making and learning from his mistakes. Not willing to answer his question but not wanting to be rude, I answered, "Are you from around here, Sir?"

"Used to be." He smiled a wistful smile. "I came here back in the thirties. I've lived several places, but mostly here."

"You've seen it all then, haven't you?" I was curious now. "Did you ever get to watch any of the greats play back then?"

"Well, I guess you could say so. I saw ol' Harry Gilmer back in the thirties—played tight end. Good man. And Scott Hunter—now there was a quarterback. I'll never forget the shoot-out with Archie Manning and his team, but he won us the game. I guess Pat Trammel had to be the best, though. He wasn't the biggest or the fastest, couldn't really do anything . . . but win. Then there was my friend Gene. You've heard of him, haven't you, Son?"

"Oh, Gene Stallings? Yes Sir!"

He continued, "Yeah, Gene was defensive coordinator. Left in '68 to go to Texas A and M. Did well out there too, but he was like me. He had to come back. It wasn't all good times, though. I remember two straight 6-5 seasons. People talked. Thought the Bear had lost his touch. Then we got the wishbone offense from a man named Royal and his staff. The Tide opened up the next season against Southern Cal, the #1 ranked team in America, and won 20-17. That score sounds familiar, doesn't it, Son? Yeah, that was in 1970. I make it back here when I can now, most years at homecoming. What about you?"

"Oh, I grew up loving Alabama. My daddy taught me football before I started school. We used to pass and kick in the yard. I played some in junior high, but I got a job after that and my playing days were over. Not that I lost interest, though. Daddy and I always watched the games or listened to them on the radio. He never got to a game at Bryant-Denny, though. As much as he loved it, he never got here. I sure wish he could have been here today." Why was I telling this to a stranger? "I feel so bad because I loved my dad, and Alabama really meant something to him. I should have made sure he got here but there was always work to be done or something that got in the way. Then he got sick and he couldn't. Now he's gone. The opportunity is gone."

Guilt washed over me like a huge wave. I shook my head; I cleared my throat; I adjusted my cap. I couldn't cry in front of a stranger.

"Son," the man replied, "I've been around for a while and I've learned a few things. One thing I know for sure is that you can't go on and on regretting the past. When the clock runs out, the game's over—you just shake it off and decide to go forward. God Almighty has given you each new day—'His mercies are new every morning'—do what you can in it. Believe me, your daddy would tell you the same thing. Just think about what you need to do now and do it. Everything will be OK. The secret is not to miss any more opportunities."

I thought about my wife, my kids, my friends, waiting for me. "I understand. Thank you."

He slapped me on the shoulder and got up. "Gotta go now. Take care, and remember, no regrets." As he walked away, he placed his Houndstooth hat back on his head. I smiled. Why hadn't I realized?

"Hey Coach," I called. He turned around. "Tell Daddy I said hello." He nodded, then walked off across the quadrangle and into the darkness as I watched in awe.

Shaking off my regrets, I stood and headed in the opposite direction toward the motel. My opportunities were waiting.

A Bellaire Ghost Story

Beverly R. Green and Brooke Moore

IT'S OCTOBER. YOU CAN FEEL IT IN THE SCHOOL. THE rickety heating system can be heard on cold days, shaking and clanking the pipes. There are unexplainable drafts—did someone leave a window open?—and the third floor ceiling is leaking. The smell of sharks in bags and dogs in barrels drifts down the staircase. The cats are still in boxes as the anatomy students run to class in white coats.

From 7:30 in the morning until 2:30 in the afternoon Monday through Friday, the events of the school day fill the halls, stacked upon the shoulders of students like the overweight book bags they carry. For seven hours, stressed teenagers laugh, cry, and learn. They memorize, hypothesize, and summarize. With both fear and excitement they struggle into adulthood while still clinging to scraps of childhood.

After school, it's time for practice. Drill and run, throw and catch. The motions are so similar to the games they used to play—tag with friends, fetch with the dog, pass with Dad—but the smiles are fewer and laughs are rare. The goal is to win, not their friend's grin, their dog's wagging tail, or their dad's high five.

Hours later, the students and athletes, teachers and staff, have all gone home. The sun has already set and brown leaves skitter across the sidewalks that surround the silent building. Windows with half drawn shades on the brick façade look like eyes with drooping lids, ready to doze off with the rest of the small, sleepy town. Inside, the halls are empty, right? The glass of the front doors is oily and opaque, so you can't see inside. Light from the street lamp is reflected from the glass, but reveals nothing.

You hesitate for a moment, then mount the steps as you did every morning of your school years. Instinctively your hand reaches for the door. It clicks. Someone has forgotten to lock this one. You dare to enter, but question the wisdom of it. Through the doors, the hall seems familiar, but in a strange, disconcerting way. Like the negative of a photograph, the structure is there but it's not the same. How long has it been? Too long, probably.

As though in a trance, you move slowly toward the middle staircase. Anything could be around that corner. Down the stairs might as well not even exist, it's so dark. You begin to climb. A soft, rhythmic noise, sort of like a scratch and a click at the same time, comes from the lower hall. Is it getting closer? The urge to run up the stairs and take them three at a time is there, but you're not as young as you were the last time you were here and you might fall.

Instead, carefully, you feel your way up to the second floor, your footsteps nearly silent. You get goosebumps as you peek around the corner. A little light from outside seeps through the windows. You can see nothing unusual. As you step forward, something soft touches your hand. Heart pounding, breath held, you back up against the wall and look around. Your shirt sleeve is sort of soft; that must be what you felt. With quickening breaths and a racing pulse, you turn right and gather the courage to walk past the lockers. Why are you doing this? Why did you come back and what are you looking for?

The colorful locks on the metal locker doors and the decorations on the walls are all gray-washed in the dim light. You know they're green and white, still the same after all these years. As you reach the end of the hall, you have the choice to return to the first floor or go up. You keep looking over your shoulder, half expecting someone to be there breathing down your neck. You choose to go up.

On the stairs again, mounting silently and slowly, you catch the sharp smell of dissection preservation chemicals. You breathe it in and out and in again slowly. It sounds strange, like two recordings playing at once. You hold your breath, but the sound continues beside you. You know something is there, but your stare is fixed down the length of the hall. Many pairs of eyes stare back.

A witness, unable to react, you recognize the shapes forming in the hallway ahead. Big and small cats and dogs jump and run and spin. Scarred tomcats and brutish pit bulls play side-by-side. None of them fight because they have nothing to be afraid of anymore. A school of sharks swims on the currents of the air, followed by tiny shark pups. The cacophony of barks and yowls slowly comes into focus in your ears as a wagging tail taps your leg repeatedly.

You scratch the dog's back, and it looks up at you. It appears very alive and normal, although its eyes shine with their own light even in shadow. Those eyes shine from within. Its feet barely brush the floor. The weightlessness of the animals makes them graceful. Excited at your touch, the dog reaches to lick your hand. He rolls around happily as you pet him, and you actually smile. You are on your knees when a silk-soft cat brushes your elbow. Three tiny kittens stumble after her. You run your free hand down the arched back of the soft cat. She purrs and a calm washes over you.

Now you know why you came back. In your hectic adult life, you have missed their presence and their tranquil touch that got you through those four long years of high school. You never knew until now, but they gave you much needed confidence and quietness of spirit during your youth. In your chaotic adult world, this peace is what you have been searching for. If you were to share the secret, would anyone believe you?

*   *   *

With sunlight streaming through the windows of the third floor, uniformed teenagers drift to class. One girl waits to enter the classroom because she is self-conscious about her looks that day. All she feels is the current of warm air brushing by her, but strangely she feels a little more confident. Brutus, once a massive dog, likes to lend students the strength to get to class and secretly scare away some bullies. This is another chance to protect a friend. An anxiety-ridden boy hides in the bathroom for a few minutes during class. He doesn't hear the purrs, but he takes a deep, calming breath and walks out the door feeling less worried. Fluffy and her kittens do a lot of good just brushing by to relieve stress. A girl who is sad because of a break-up feels a giggle bubble up inside as a school of sharks circles her and swims off on the air. The little laugh brings her hope that tomorrow will be a better day.

The animals come and go through the years just like the students, but some of them like to stick around. They help when and how they can using the gifts that are innately theirs. The sharks are always excited about something, the dogs are playful and loyal, and the cats are confident and calm. When students hear the patter of footsteps somewhere down the hall, or something brushing against a locker door, they never guess the source of the sound. Unknown and unseen, the animals from the anatomy class offer peace and support.

The Thing in the Road

THERE HAD NOT BEEN MUCH EXCITEMENT IN THE TINY, faded, coal mine town of Bella Donna, Ohio for many years. In its heyday it had never been an imposing place, but since the decline of the mining industry, Bella Donna's general store, post office, gas station and alterations shop had closed, leaving a biker bar and a Greek Orthodox Church as the only hives of activity in the place. Several stately houses had once existed in the town, but recent years found them empty and weighted down by heavy vines that grew like unkempt graying hair upon their aging heads and faces. Smaller homes were owned and occupied, mostly by elderly people or those whose families had always lived in Bella Donna and could not bear to give up on the memory of the place. No more school buses made the early morning pick-ups or late afternoon deposits. There had been no school-aged children in Bella Donna to ride them for several years, not since the youngest of the Paoletti children learned to drive. A small creek ran through the town area, often turned orange by feeders leaking from the deserted mines. However, as it continued out of town its waters cleared up and paralleled a little-known, lovely country lane bordered on both sides by hard woods, then hills that bristled with pines. The mood of the place was often dreary, but if one were to look beyond his walls, he might find a natural beauty in the landscape that changed with the seasons and brought a little brightness.

Of late, commercial quantities of oil and natural gas had been located in the area, and frackers and rig workers moved in, disrupting the peace of the community. New extended cab pick-up trucks began to outnumber the motorcycles parked outside the bar. Eighteen wheelers ran the roads through all hours carrying in drill bits, pump jacks, cranes, poles, and coil tubing. Huge tankers carried out liquids, sludge and slurry. The formerly sleepy roads became animated with giant vehicles that were unable to safely negotiate them. Their sheer weight caused parts of the roads to fall away and pot holes to appear. There were many near accidents.

Nick Paoletti was twenty-four years old. He had grown up in Bella Donna in a home with his coal miner father, stay-at-home mother, and four siblings, two brothers and two sisters: Rocco, Giuseppe (Joe), Rosie, and Silvia. Niccolo, or Nick, was next to the youngest. All were graduates of St. James Central Catholic School, Kindergarten through high school, which was located several miles down the road in Martinsville. There he had played sports and made the honor roll and invested in many friendships. Intelligent, charismatic, good-looking, and full of potential, Nick had made plans to attend Ohio University after graduation, but sometimes life deals an unfair hand and finances and the needs of his family due to his father's long illness and eventual death sent him to the coal mines with hopes of attending one of the local junior colleges when time permitted.

One calm October night, fifty-two degrees with stars crowding to peek around the clouds that seemed to glow in the light of the moon, Nick was driving home down the Bella Donna road, radio in his '98 red Ford pick-up truck blaring old time rock-and-roll. Suddenly, the leaf-strewn terrain on either side of the road began to blur as a misplaced cloud passed before the headlights. He had just passed the quarry when suddenly, a figure appeared shrouded in the fog on the road, ghostly white in the diffused moonlight. Caught by complete surprise, Nick hit the brakes and swerved to the left to miss the not-really-human figure. He braced himself for impact with the trees but none came. He also did not end up in a ditch.

Opening his eyes (which he did not realize he had closed) and taking a breath (which he did not realize he was holding), Nick found himself on a narrow, dirt track between the trees. In all the years he had traveled this road as passenger or driver, he had never noticed this appendage. Curiosity was not enough to overcome his shock and relief at the moment and he stored the information for later, reversed the truck back onto the main road, and travelled the remaining ten minutes home.

When he arrived, the old, two-story, frame house was nearly dark. Everyone else was in bed. His mother, God bless her, had left a plate of pasta and garlic bread covered with plastic wrap on the kitchen counter. Without warming it or sitting down, Nick leaned against the counter and slowly ate the dinner thinking: *What in the world had happened out there? Was he so tired that he was hallucinating? Not likely. What was that thing in the road?*

The next day dawned sunny and warm, another perfect October day. In the daylight it was possible to dismiss the occurrence of the night before, even though he could not explain it. He had a little time since he was on second shift and his younger sister Silvia (who also still lived at home) was at work and his mother was out shopping, so Nick decided to go check out that mysterious dirt road. It was a little hard to find, but knowing the area as he did, Nick finally discovered the narrow entrance between the golden-leafed trees. Carefully he followed the tracks that had obviously not been travelled for some time. At one point he had to stop the truck and get out to remove a small fallen tree from across the path. This drive seemed a little darker than the main road because of the density of the trees which still held on to most of their leaves. Abruptly, the path dead-ended into a brick wall with a wrought-iron gate. There was a chain and a lock on the gate. The wall was not high, so Nick hopped out of his truck to see what might be beyond it. A strange chill went down his spine. It was an old, overgrown cemetery. He could see obelisks and Celtic crosses rising above the tall weeds.

The lock on the gate was rusted tight. Nick looked around carefully, then vaulted over the wall to get a closer look. Spreading the dried weeds with his hands, he could see that the grave stones were very old and weathered. Some had fallen over and some were crumbling. The only surname he could make out was McDonald, and the only full name was Silas McDonald. It was probably a family cemetery, but Nick remembered no McDonalds ever living in Bella Donna.

Very odd indeed, but it was time for him to return home and get ready for work. Backing down the dirt road was not nearly as easy as going forward and Nick found himself in a ditch. *I must have been crazy coming out here alone* he thought as pewter clouds covered the sun and the wind began to blow. Nick put the old Ford in neutral and pushed until he liberated it from the ditch. He jumped back in and put the truck in gear. It slung back onto the old road in an arc of mud and leaves. Rain began to fall and still he drove in reverse. Like emerging from the underworld, the truck exited the last of the tree canopy and Nick was on the pavement again, sweaty, dirty, and late.

After work, Nick played with the thought of going home another way, but his young mind made fun of that idea and he turned onto the Bella Donna road. He arrived home that night with no incidents beyond dodging the eighteen-wheelers coming from the pump station. His mother was still up.

"Mom!" he hugged her with devotion. Nick was very close to his fifty-five-year-old, Italian mother.

"Tesoro! Are you hungry?" short but sturdy Rose Paoletti asked, pride for her son evident in her chocolate-brown eyes.

"Yes, I am! What are we having?"

"Polenta with cheese."

It wasn't Nick's favorite, but he was grateful as his mother placed the warm food and a glass of tea on the table in front of him. "Thanks, Mom," he said and she patted him on the shoulder in response. "Can I ask you a question?"

"Certainly, Caro. Anything."

"Do you remember there ever being a family named McDonald living around here?"

"No, I don't think so. Why?" She sat down next to him at the table.

"Just wondered. Did you know there was a path out to an old cemetery off the Bella Donna road near the quarry?"

"Niccolo, what have you been up to?" Rose pushed her gray-streaked hair back away from her face revealing an expression of concern.

"Nothing, Mom. I promise. Nothing for you to worry about." He patted her hand and smiled. He certainly did not intend to cause her worry.

As Nick headed to bed that night, he noticed his mother's bedroom light was still on. The door was open just a crack and he could hear her voice. Not wanting to intrude, but a little concerned, Nick leaned closer to the door. Rose was praying her rosary.

Life went on as usual after that for nearly a month. The weather changed and it was nearly always cold. The trees dropped their leaves and those drab, frosty days between the brilliance of autumn and the first snowfall arrived. Plans began to be made for Thanksgiving.

One night, Nick was headed home preoccupied with thoughts of seeing Rocco, Joe and Rosie and their families soon, of how much fun it always was to have a big dinner together followed by touch football out in the yard, and of having everyone back in the same house together. Fog had begun to roll in. He had just passed the quarry when there in the headlights, an ominous, pale, inhuman figure appeared! As before, Nick braked the truck and swerved to the left and under the trees onto the cemetery road. Heart beating fast, he jumped out of the truck and ran back to the main road. Nothing was there. Nothing. The filmy fog rolled silently across the road and the only sound was that of his engine still running. Upset, Nick went back to the truck, reversed it onto the pavement, and headed home. That time he said nothing about it to anyone.

When the family came in for Thanksgiving, Nick tried to immerse himself in the activity, but sometimes his mind still went back to the thing in the road. Thanksgiving night after all the bustle was over and most of the family had gone off to bed, Nick and Joe remained companionably awake in the living room. They watched football highlights on television and commented on the games and the coming basketball season and memories of childhood. When the opportunity presented itself Nick asked, "Do you remember any McDonalds who lived around here when we were kids?"

"Don't think so. Why?"

"I just happened to find this old cemetery back in the woods off the Bella Donna road. Most of the stones had the name McDonald on them."

"Must have been from pretty far back. What were you doing out in the woods off the Bella Donna road?"

Nick hesitated. "If I tell you, you're going to think I'm crazy."

"I already think you're crazy."

Nick threw a couch pillow at his brother.

"Hey!" Joe teased "I'll tell Mom. Seriously, what happened?"

Joe listened as Nick unfolded his experiences with the thing in the road.

"Wow! Don't know what to say about that. Thanks for not telling Mom, though. She worries enough. Tell you what: We'll drive over there tomorrow morning before I leave and have a look."

"Thanks, Joe." Nick slept a little better that night just for having told someone else.

The next morning after Rocco and his family had headed back home and Rosie and her girls, Joe's wife, and Silvia joined Rose for their annual Black Friday shopping excursion, the brothers headed out on the first adventure they had taken together since they were boys. The fog was thick on the Bella Donna road and it took some looking to find the break in the trees. They were in Joe's new SUV and he wasn't sure he wanted to take it down a long-abandoned path with ditches and ruts, so they parked just off the main road and walked. It was farther than Nick remembered. They trudged without talking over the fog-sodden brown leaves and gravel, skeletal tree limbs grabbing at their jackets from time to time.

"Are you sure this is the right road?" Joe asked.

Nick nodded. "Yeah." He pointed out the ditch where his truck had become stuck. The disturbance in the ground was still visible.

Joe glanced at his watch. Then they spotted the wrought iron gate and the brick wall. The lock was still in place.

"How'd you get in?"

Nick smiled and demonstrated how he placed his hands on top of the low wall, pulled up and vaulted over.

"You can't be serious! You're asking an awful lot of this ol' man."

"Haha. Come on, ol' man."

Joe struggled over the wall.

"It's strange." Nick observed. "Someone's been here. The grave sites have been cleared off."

Sure enough, the tall, cumbersome weeds that had covered many of the stones had been cut down and tossed into a burn pile in the corner. The grass was brown but cut short and the leaves had been cleared. Most of the stones were still tumbled and worn except for the tall Celtic crosses and obelisks which looked like ominous guardians. Most of the stones held the name McDonald.

"I'll be!" Joe was amazed. "I never would have known this was here. Thought we'd been all over these woods when we were kids. Hmph."

They looked around for a little longer. The sun got higher and the fog lifted, so the walk back to the SUV was a lot more pleasant. "All I can tell ya, Bro," Joe advised on the way back, "is to be very aware on the drive home at night. Can't imagine what you're seeing on the road. It's weird; be careful."

"Thanks," Nick answered. *That's no help,* is what he thought.

Holiday over and back to work: nothing out of the ordinary happened. Christmas came and garish porch decorations cast odd shadows everywhere, but nothing disturbing arose from those shadows and although it crossed his mind from time to time, the thing in the road no longer intruded on Nick's thoughts.

Then one sunny afternoon Nick was returning from a batch of day-off errands—run to the barber for a haircut, run to Walmart for orange juice and new socks, run the truck through the car wash to remove the caked on salt and grit—when he noticed another red pick-up turning off the main road to the right just past the quarry near the spot where the mysterious figure had twice appeared. The truck's movement down the unpaved road was quickly hidden by the trees.

"Wonder where that path ends up," Nick spoke to himself. On a whim, he followed the truck. It led him down a slight hill toward the creek, then along the water's edge, across a small wooden bridge, and up to a house with a barn and large area that appeared to have been a corn field. A paddock kept four horses, three brown and one white. An old man exited the pick-up and waited for Nick.

"Afternoon. Can I help you?" the old man asked as Nick approached and they shook hands.

"I'm Nick Paoletti. I live in Bella Donna. Never realized there was anything back here."

"Jeremiah McDonald. Lived out here all my life—my family's farm."

"Wait. You're name's McDonald and this is your farm."

"Yep, and don't say it. I've heard it all, heheh,"

"You don't know of a Silas McDonald by any chance, do you?"

"He was my grandfather. How do you know about Silas?"

Nick got brave. "That must be your family's cemetery on the other side of the road out in the woods."

"Sure is. I saw it looked like someone had been back there."

"I didn't mean to intrude. It's just that my brother and I roamed all over this area when we were boys and it's surprising that we never discovered it before."

"What led you back in those woods?"

"Well, to be honest, there was something out in the road when I was coming home one night, two nights actually, and when I swerved to miss it, I ended up on that road. Glad it was there. Thought I was going to run into a tree."

"Was the thing in the road big and kind of ghostly looking?"

"Yes! Have you seen it, too?"

"Come over here, Nick," Jeremiah said as he led Nick over to the fence. "Angel!" he called. The gray-white horse walked to the fence and affectionately nuzzled Jeremiah's jacket. Jeremiah responded by reaching over the fence and rubbing her face and neck. "Yeah, that's a good ol' girl," he spoke gently to the horse. Things were coming into a comforting focus for Nick. "She's a good horse, Nick, but she's really old and I think she's got kind of senile. For some reason she's taken to getting out and wandering off at night. Imagine she's what you saw in the road. I'm sorry. Glad she didn't cause an accident. There's enough out there to have to dodge with those confounded trucks without adding a crazy horse to the mix."

"Mr. McDonald, I can't tell you how glad I am to meet you and Angel. I thought I was losing my mind. It has been very good to meet you both. I'll let you get back to what you need to do, but thank you for the answers."

"You're welcome, Nick. Good to meet you, Son."

"Have a good day, Sir."

Nick got back in his truck, his mood as light as the air. He was singing as he walked into the house and he stopped and hugged his mother who was running the vacuum over their worn, print, living room rug. She laughed and responded, "Dinner in an hour, Niccolo."

That evening he called Joe and told his brother the story.

"Well I guess that's it then. Glad the mystery is solved," Joe said.

"I guess so," Nick responded and wondered why he no longer felt convinced.

No matter how hard we try, some things just won't be put to rest until they're ready to be put to rest. A night arrived in March, and as usual, Nick was driving home from his shift at the mine. The fog was very thick and became more so as he turned down the Bella Donna road. Slowing a bit to deal with the weather, Nick passed the quarry. Suddenly, the thing in the road! "Angel!" he yelled and jerked the wheel to the left without fear onto the now familiar cemetery road.

Nearly as soon as he made the turn, Nick heard an explosion and saw a ball of fire rise above the trees close enough that he could feel the heat. He pulled out his cell phone and quickly dialed 911 even as he ran back toward the main road. An oil tanker coming from the well had apparently suffered a collision with one of the old trees that grew close to the road. *This road never was wide enough for those trucks,* Nick thought. As he watched the flames spread to the woods, the Bella Donna Volunteer Fire Department arrived followed by other first-responders. They began to battle the flames, and Nick dialed home.

"Nick?" It was Silvia.

"Yes, it's me. I'm fine. The accident was just ahead of me. I was saved by an Angel."

"Niccolo!" Now his mother was on the phone.

"I love you, Mom. I'll come home through St. Catherine. I'll see you soon."

Shaken, Nick watched for a moment longer. Then he turned his truck around and headed for home. He really had been saved by an Angel!

The next day, Nick called to tell Joe about this new chapter of his bizarre story. Joe repeated Nick's thoughts from the night before. "You were saved by an Angel, Baby Brother."

Nick left early for work in order to stop by the McDonald farm. When he arrived, Jeremiah greeted him on the porch. "Nick! Glad to see you safe! That was quite a fire last night!"

Nick reached out and shook Mr. McDonald's hand enthusiastically. "Mr. McDonald, I don't know just how much you've heard about what happened on the road last night, but I owe Angel my life. I would have been in that collision if she hadn't been out in the road and made me turn off. I think she must be psychic."

"What do you mean, Nick?" Mr. McDonald had a strange look on his face.

"Angel. She must have gotten out again last night. I saw her in the same place as usual and I turned off on the cemetery road to miss her just as the collision took place. If she hadn't been out there, I would have been right in the middle of that crash."

"Nick, Angel's been dead for about a month. Whatever was out in the road last night wasn't her."

A chill went up Nick's spine as he looked at the paddock. Angel was not there.

Never again did Nick see the thing in the road. Never again did he talk about it. When Joe asked him about it once, Nick just brushed off the question: "Haven't seen that horse in a long time." But he thought about it often, especially on those foggy nights as he drove home from work just past the quarry. Horse? Ghost? Angel? Whatever it was had saved his life and he was forever grateful.

A WALK IN THE DARK

Tall Tales

Beverly R. Green
(from Carry My Tears to Shiloh,
Ichthus Publications, 2018.)

AS SPRING PASSED INTO SUMMER AND THE SONG OF THE cicadas filled the air night and day, Turtle, Tad and Jobie became very good friends. The brothers taught the newcomer Jobie the workings of the Maghee farm, and Jobie jumped right in and worked side by side with the rest of the family. He began to smile more often and talk much more often, and he loved to tell stories.

One very hot, breezeless night, Turtle and Tad decided to go to the barn loft and sleep with Jobie to escape the close, stuffy air of the house. They knew the large, open hay door allowed more fresh air to enter, and the larger space allowed for circulation. That was the excuse anyway. Really they just wanted to have time to talk with Jobie about adventures and other boy stuff.

Turtle and Tad sneaked out quietly and ran as silently as they could to the dark, forbidding barn. "It sure looks diff'rent out here at night, Turtle," Tad remarked in a nervous whisper.

The barn door creaked eerily as they opened it, and again as they closed it. They had to make their way very carefully across the floor to the ladder. Turtle went first, and Tad followed by the sound of Turtle's steps more than by sight.

"Here's the ladder," Turtle finally whispered, and he began to climb. Tad stretched out his arm in front of him until he touched a rung near the bottom, and he also started to climb. They had just reached the top and started making their way across the floor of the loft when, clink, Tad's foot bumped something. Like a shot, up jumped Jobie with a pitch fork in his hands ready to strike. In the moonlight, the brothers could see his threatening silhouette.

"Jobie! It's us!" a startled Turtle said in what was *not* a whisper as Tad jumped behind his brother for safety.

"Taaaar-nation!" Jobie responded, lowering the pitch fork. "Turtle? That you? Tad? I thought maybe you was the Skeleton of Meaty Bones come to eat my skin off."

"The what?" Turtle and Tad looked at each other.

"The Skeleton of Meaty Bones. I done met him in the woods when I was makin' my way here."

"That ain't true!" Tad barked, but he wasn't sure.

"Is true!"

"What happened then if it's so true?"

"Well si' down and I'll tell ya."

Alice had made a nice home for Jobie up there and it was almost unfair to call his side of it a hay loft any longer. There was a cot with a down mattress and pillow, a multi-colored quilt, a brown blanket, a small rough board table with two ladder-back chairs and an oil lamp, a cup and a plate. Beside the cot was a wash stand with a white bowl and pitcher and a towel. There were hooks on the wall where Jobie could hang his few belongings. As their eyes became accustomed to the diffused moonlight in the loft, Turtle and Tad looked enviously around the little abode. They each took a seat at the table.

Jobie began: "I was walkin' in the woods. Don't know what time it was, but reckon it was aroun' midnight—the time when all the haints comes out. All of a sudden, I starts hearin' footsteps behin' me, and a kind of rattlin'."

"Rattlin'?"

"Hush, Tad! What was it, Jobie?"

"I turns aroun', real careful-like, and there is the biggest skeleton I ever seed. Bigger than a growed man. And his teeths look like a big grin acrossed his face. And his eyes was a-glowin' with a light from inside his hade.

"'Who is you?' I asked, cause I had never seed nothin' like that befo', bones a-walkin' aroun' on they own with no skin coverin' 'em.

"'I's the Skeleton of Meaty Bones and I's gonna eat you up, so's I kin put some meat on my bones.' He says an' he laughs a terrible laugh.

"'Oh, no, you ain't,' says I, and I takes off runnin'.

"So the Skeleton of Meaty Bones call for his brothers, Starkin and Hairkin, and they all begin to chase me through them woods. Purty soon, Starkin was right behin' me, but I ducks under a low hangin' branch, and Starkin' runs slap dab into it and knocks 'is hade clean off 'is neck and falls down dade!"

Turtle and Tad laughed at that.

"Then here come Hairkin right behin' me, so I runs to a big rock hangin' over a loooooong drop. It was so far down and I almos' fell down it myself, but I move out the way jus' in time, and Hairkin went a-fallin' over the edge and 'is bones busted all apart down below."

The boys laughed again.

"So then it was jus' me and the Skeleton of Meaty Bones, and he come a-chasin' me through them woods a-shoutin' . . ."

Jobie didn't have time to finish, because at that moment a booming voice came from the ladder saying, "I come to eat all of ye up and put meat on my bones!"

The three boys jumped up and ran to the back of the loft trying desperately to find a place to hide! Stitch began to bark hysterically from the floor below! All of a sudden, the story seemed to have become true!

Then came laughter, and it was laughter they all recognized. A light appeared in a lantern, and there was Abel, standing at the top of the ladder in his long johns and hat, with tears pouring down his face from uncontrollable amusement. "Y'all's faces!" He just kept repeating, "Y'all's faces!"

"Grampaw!" The boys yelled.

"How did you know we were here?" Turtle asked.

"Y'all didn't think ye could sneak out the house without somebody hearin' ye, did ye?"

"You heard us?" Tad was amazed. Both boys had thought their grandfather was becoming a bit hard-of-hearing.

"Weeeeeeeelllllll, no, it weren't exactly me heard ye," Abel admitted. "It was yer maw, and she come and woke me up and told me to foller ye."

That sounded more credible. They could never hide anything from their maw.

"Was she mad, Grampaw?" Tad was feeling guilty.

"Naw. She just didn't know where y'all were headed and she didn't want anybody to git hurt." He sat down on the hay and tossed a bag of nuts out in front of him. The boys scrambled to get some, amazed at this unexpected treat. They all sat down with their grandfather around the lamp and chomped. "It is nice and cool up here, ain't it?"

The boys nodded.

"You tell us a story, Grampaw," Turtle said.

"A story? Let me see . . . a story . . . 'Bout twenty year ago I was a-fishin' down at the narrow end of the lake. All of a sudden, the biggest black bear I done ever seen walks down to the bank acrossed from me. We was only about thirty yards from each other, so I seen 'im good and I seen what happened real good, too.

"Well, that bear come into the water and commenced a-fishin'. Fish after fish he caught on his claws and slung 'em up on the bank 'til he had ten big fish. Guess he figured that was enough cause he come up out the water a-lickin' his chops and ready to eat.

"Suddenly, out of the woods come this huge critter, all furry and 'bout ten feet tall. It had ten arms a-wavin'in the air and a little, tiny head with some big ol' teeth in it. It was a-hissin' and a-screechin' to high heaven. Well that bear, he stood lookin' in shock for a minute, then he takes off into the woods leavin' all his fish behind." The boys laughed at that.

Abel continued, "As soon as the bear was gone, the critter got quiet, and then . . . it begin to come apart! Dad-gum if it weren't five raccoons stacked up on each other's shoulders, tails wrapped around 'em hidin' their faces, 'cept for the one on top. Each one of them raccoons run and grabbed one fish in its mouth and another fish in its hands, and off they run on two feet like little people.

"Yep, that poor bear went hungry that day, but the raccoons et purdy good." The boys were literally rolling on the floor laughing by the end of the tale.

"Time to sleep now, boys," Abel announced. "The sun'll be up early and we need to be up with it." He lay back in the hay, and before long they were all snoring.

A WALK IN THE DARK

Our Parents' Gift

Beverly R. Green and E. L. Risden

THE EVENING FELT PERFECT: A LOVELY RESTAURANT, beautiful flowers, soft music, glowing candles, *Fettuccine Aglio e Olio* (easy on the garlic) with a bottle of Marlborough Sauvignon Blanc, even a handsome escort in a suit and tie. Dr. Abraham Fox, the new head of the History Department at the local college, was certainly the most promising date that Holly Graham had experienced in quite a while.

Holly was good-looking, fifty-nine years old, reasonably well off, and single. She had gathered master's degrees in a bouquet of diplomas. More interested in collecting and studying art objects and antiquities than in teaching, she had never bothered to complete a PhD. But when the dean asked her, Holly would offer the occasional course in art history, restoration, curatorial practices, and, when the campus Classicist was on sabbatical, she'd take on first- and second-year Latin.

Following an unfortunate romantic adventure involving a young anthropology professor, she had refused for years to date members of the faculty: she hated the fluent and often vitriolic gossip that tainted academic life. Dates were getting harder and harder to come by as Holly neared sixty, and she did not particularly fancy old age alone. She'd gone through times of trying to find a mate, but Holly's unusual hobbies usually shook her clear of the dating trail: in addition to assembling a wall full of diplomas, she bought and sold antiques, practiced all four main family styles of *taiji chuan*, wrote children's stories, and refurbished and translated old manuscripts. Along with credentials amply displayed on the wall of her home office, she kept another mound of diplomas in a desk drawer to save wall space for more interesting decorations. She had completed master's study in Art History, Classics, Eastern European History, Celtic Studies, and Archeology, plus acquired certificates of accomplishment in Herbology, Viticulture and Enology, and *Enigmatology*—an undergraduate major she had designed herself to allow her to pursue whatever odd texts and objects interested her. As pleasant, informed, and attractive as she was, Holly's intellect proved too much for most suitors, who feared they couldn't keep up with her intelligence or her energy. But not Abraham Fox: he had as much curiosity and as varied interests as Holly—an unsual find indeed.

"Abraham, won't you come in," Holly offered when they got back to her house after dinner. "I've just got a few new antiquities that might interest you: some South-American potshards, a Mesopotamian fertility doll, and some beautiful original Japanese *sumi-e* paintings."

She winced. It sounded like a variation of the cheap, old line, "Would you like to come up and see my etchings?" or worse, an invitation to a scholarly lecture. To her surprise, Abraham smiled and nodded yes. They had filled their evening with plenty of academic conversation, but Holly's collection had a reputation, and Abraham felt eager to see whatever she considered new and interesting.

Holly took Abraham's coat at the door and hung it neatly in the front closet. Then she led him down a hardwood hallway and switched on a light. She had converted two of the three bedrooms in the house into a small museum. Glass-topped display cases inhabited the middle of each room while shelves reached from floor to ceiling showing off beautiful rocks and crystals, pottery vessels, wooden as well as metal tools, iron and steel weapons, arrowheads, ancient coins, pieces of old documents scratched in strange glyphs, and all manner of interesting treasures. Abraham was amazed. He perused the shelves with interest, carefully lifting something here and there to study or admire it.

"The new pieces are on my desk," Holly said. "I haven't finished categorizing and labelling them yet."

"I'm beyond words," Abraham finally said. Then his eyes lighted on a piece of a broken, apparently formerly round, gray plate that hung on the wall. "Tell me about this."

"Until recently that was my favorite piece," Holly smiled. She gently removed it from the wall. Speaking in a very quiet, almost reverent voice she explained, "Everything in these two rooms I've dug up, in one way or another, on my own, except for this one. My father was stationed in France during the Second World War. He brought this home and cherished it although I've never fully understood why." Holly caressed the piece of broken plate before she handed it to Abraham.

He received it with fascination, running his fingers over the rough, raised portions of the plate. "There are letters here around the rim."

"Yes."

"*I, T, A,* then a space, then *V, I, A* . . . Latin? Something *way*? What does it mean?"

"I've had ideas about it, but just recently something's come up to throw them into doubt."

Abraham turned the piece over. "There's something on the back, too. Some kind of diagram."

"Yes."

"Holly, you may have something of real importance here. Do you know what it is? And you say you've found something even more interesting than this?"

"I once thought I'd identified it with pretty fair certainty." She reached for the piece, and he returned it reluctantly. She carefully replaced it in its bracket on the wall. There was an awkward pause.

"Well, then," Abraham smiled, "thank you for a most enjoyable evening. But it's late, and I shouldn't keep you any longer."

Sadly, Holly walked him to the door and returned his coat—the evening seemed to her to be coming to too abrupt an ending. "Thank you, Abraham. I had a lovely time."

He took her hand and kissed her on the cheek, lingering briefly. He had barely noticed her perfume earlier: quite nice. "*Lauren*? It's just right for you. Very present, but still a little mysterious. We'll talk again soon, I hope?"

Holly smiled and nodded. She opened the door, and he left, turning to wave at her as he walked away.

Alone in the house, Holly kicked off her shoes and walked back to the display rooms to turn out the lights. Instead, she almost absent-mindedly returned to the plate fragment. She removed it once again from the wall and carried it to her bedroom. There she pulled a box out of the closet. She knew its contents well, but kept it hidden, not part of her wall displays. She drew from the box an artifact in bubble wrap with a note from an old friend whose father had served alongside hers in France. She had read the note a dozen times, but, feeling lonesome, she read it again:

"I don't know if this shard is anything of value, but I know you love artifacts. I found it among my father's possessions after he died, among things he brought back from overseas, and I immediately thought of you. If you don't want it, feel free to dispose of it. Call me sometime. It would be fun to catch up. Marcia 412-233-6478."

Marcia had been a good pal all the way back to early college days, but this gift, something from her father, was special indeed. Holly carefully opened the bubble wrap. Inside was a fragment, also apparently broken from a round, gray plate. It had the same type of rough, raised letters along the side. She fit it next to her piece from the wall. The letters V, E, and R were visible on the rim and she traced them all with her finger as she had done many times before. "I, T, A, space, V, I, A, very small space, then just below V, E, R. Yes, she had a clear idea of what it said: "Via, Veritas, Vita" — "the way, the truth, and the life." Perhaps it had just been a modest, devotional bread plate, but Holly was convinced that there was more. What was the strange diagram on the back? Did the rest of the plate, about a third of which was still missing, exist somewhere? How she wished she could find it! The perfect size and shape for a paten, probably medieval . . . Not going to solve it tonight, she thought — better get some sleep.

Holly lay in bed for a time unable to sleep. Finally she got up, pulled on an old pair of jeans and a sweatshirt, put on a coat and a cap from the front closet, and went out for a walk. Her street was well lit, and during occasional bouts of insomnia she'd walk to a cozy park only a couple blocks from her house where a group of college students often gathered for all-night sessions of acoustic guitar, bongos, and scat singing. She found them at it under a streetlamp by the old stone fountain, and she sat down at a bench nearby and listened. One of the students looked over and waved for her to join them, but she just waved back and nodded a "go ahead" and remained where she was, comfortably listening in the shadows.

She followed strings of recognizable melodies that folded themselves around the bongo patter, dropping to make room for improvised vocals that rose and fell from one singer to another. One sounded like an alto sax, followed by a soft tenor who dueled rhythms with the bongo player. Then somebody mimicked a bass fiddle, who gave way to a young woman with a very deep voice doing a French horn, and then another with a soprano be-bop and a then a young man who whistled like a bamboo flute—the sounds, flitting like moths under the lamplight, took Holly to the very edge of pleasant sleep.

And there before her stood her father, looking as he did in his healthy mid-forties. He smiled lovingly.

Holly wanted to leap up and hug him, but her body wouldn't move, weighed down by sleep even as her awareness felt awake and alive.

He held up one finger, signaling for her to pay attention. Then he pulled from the pocket of his coat a thin, leather-bound book. He opened the book and displayed first one page and then another. Each had only one letter. Holly watched, attentive.

G, R, A, A, L.

Then he closed the little book and replaced it in his pocket.

He smiled again, waved his finger back and forth, and spoke.

"Not what you were thinking at first," he said. "You were right to doubt. Important, yes, but not what you were looking for. You know what I mean. You know what it is, and where: the piece you really want to find. Go find it!"

He blew her a kiss, and disappeared to wherever dreams go when they come to an end.

Holly felt someone shaking her shoulder. She opened her eyes and saw the young woman who had been singing those beautiful alto scats.

"Are you all right, ma'am?" the young woman asked. "I think you fell asleep. We were worried about you. We're going home now, and we didn't want to leave you alone."

"Thank you," Holly said. "So kind of you, and how silly of me. You're a lovely singer, you and your friends, too. I so much enjoyed listening to you."

The musicians thanked her, and Holly shook the sleep from her limbs and walked home. The sky was clear, and she could see the first hint of light over the eastern horizon.

She walked home, dropped back into bed, and fell into a deep sleep. After what she had seen in the park, she might have expected to dream again, but she didn't.

She woke and looked at the clock: already 9:00. No problem, since it was Saturday . . . She got up and made some coffee and began peeling an orange, when suddenly the dream she had in the park came back to her in full force. She shivered.

"What did he mean by that" got interrupted in her thoughts by "was that really?" and she found herself breaking into tears—every now and then the feeling would strike her of just how much she missed her father. Not a crier, Holly felt embarrassed at herself, tried to steady her thoughts, and took a large bite of orange. The strong, sour-sweet aroma and the rich, wild citrus flavor filled her senses and woke her to the idea she had only half formulated.

The word *Graal* called to mind Chrétien de Troyes. In the late twelfth-century *Conte du Graal*, Perceval desired to become a knight, but received some bad advice from Gornemant: to avoid quick speech and asking too many questions. As he set off from home, Perceval met a fisherman who sent him to a nearby castle to spend the night. In the castle he was led to a great hall where sat an old man. As he watched, a squire entered the hall carrying a sword which bore the message that it would not break except in sore peril. The old man gave the sword to Perceval and told him that it was "adjudged and destined" for him. Another squire entered carrying a bloody lance. Two more squires followed, each carrying a two-branched candlestick. Then came a damsel with a broad platter, a *grail*, in her hand that outshone the candles. A second damsel followed bearing a silver plate.

Although he wondered about it all, Perceval remembered the advice of Gornemant and did not ask questions. At supper, Perceval was given a second chance, but again refrained from questions. In the morning he awoke to find the castle deserted and his horse ready to depart. As he rode over the drawbridge, it quickly closed behind him.

The poem ended unfinished, and sadly Perceval was never able to receive his answers. But Holly was not so naive as to dismiss her questions, and her dream had incited a quest of her own.

Wolfram von Eschenbach had considered the Grail to be a stone. Robert de Boron had been the first to consider it Jesus' cup from the Last Supper. *The Queste Del Sainte Graal*, from the *Prose Launcelot* Vulgate Cycle came from the thirteenth century and refigured the story with Galahad as chief of the Grail knights. Thomas Malory's version, drawn from the *Launcelot*, became the major English version in the fifteenth century. By that time the idea of the Grail as the cup of Christ had long settled into literature and the Christian imagination. But research on the idea of the Grail had never stopped: Holly remembered reading an article by a scholar who argued the Grail was a linen, perhaps a shroud, maybe even The Shroud of Turin itself, that a Byzantine church had unveiled gradually during Lent, finally exhibiting an image of the crucified Christ on Easter morning.

"It's *a grail*," she said out loud, "but not *the* Grail," she said out loud, thinking of the grey plate fragments: like the platter in Chrétien. She held the rest of the orange in her teeth, picked up her cup and a napkin, and went to her desk. For the next two hours she rifled through her collection of medieval art history books until she finally found the passage that had been sitting just beyond the reach of her memory. It was in Professor Fundess' volume on medieval European religious artifacts.

Holly smiled and closed the volume with a thump. She dialed the number on Marcia's note. The phone rang several times, and she finally got an answering machine. Drat! Holly thought. She hadn't thought that she was calling right in the middle of day and would be lucky to catch Marcia at all. Well, not much she could do about it now . . .

Then a living voice interrupted the recorded message. "Yes, hello?"

"Marcia? This is Holly. I'm so glad I got you. I got so excited about something that I completely forgot about the time of day. Did I catch you in the middle of something?"

"Holly? Holly Graham? What a nice surprise! Where are you?"

"I'm at home. I was just wondering if I might take you up on your offer to talk."

"Uh, sure. Just let me just put these packages aside. I took my lunch hour to do some shopping, but I need to get back to work lickety-split. Can I call you back tonight?"

"I'm sorry to have caught you at a bad time. I'm really sorry about your father, too. Look, what I'd like is to talk in person. May I come to see you in Pittsburgh?"

"Of course!" Marcia said. "Is something wrong?"

"Nothing wrong at all. Just some questions I have about the package you sent and our fathers and the time they spent in France. Is next weekend too soon?"

"Next weekend would be fine. Text me the arrangements, and I'll pick you up at the airport."

"Thanks, Marcia! This means a lot to me! Oh, I hope I haven't made you late. Bye."

"Bye, Hol—so great to hear from you!"

Holly went straight to her computer to book a flight to Pittsburgh. She was so absorbed in her new adventure that she jumped when her phone rang. It was Abraham Fox!

"Holly. I had a wonderful time last night. How would you feel about getting together for lunch? Are you free?"

"Oh! Abraham! Are you sure?" It was a strange reply, but Holly was unaccustomed to enthusiastic offers of second dates.

Abraham laughed. "Well, yes, I'm sure. The weather is supposed to be nice. How would you like to bike out to the lake for a picnic?"

"That sounds wonderful," she sighed. "Yes, a picnic would be perfect."

"I'll bring lunch and meet you in front of your garage in an hour."

"You bet! I'll be ready." Holly hung up the phone and did an unpracticed version of a happy dance. Feeling a little foolish, she stopped and glared at a rare photograph of General Custer, whose eyes stared back into hers. "What are *you* looking at, George?" she questioned the photograph with a laugh as she hopped back to the computer to complete her reservation.

At exactly noon, Abraham rode into Holly's driveway, with a pack on his back, helmet on his head, and smile on his face. "Are you ready?" he asked. He was wearing knee-length khaki shorts, but had a navy-blue windbreaker since the air still felt cool.

"Absolutely!" she answered and pulled her helmet over her doubled-over, grey-brown ponytail.

"Let's go!"

Holly mounted her Martone Pacific Diamond bicycle, a purchase she had considered frivolous but for which she had been so often grateful. She loved its ocean blue color and the ease with which it held the road. Abraham kept a pleasant pace that suited Holly perfectly.

It was indeed a glorious afternoon. They peddled leisurely through the play of sun and shadow, warm and cool, beneath the trees that lined the streets on the way to the lake. They turned right onto a busier thoroughfare and rode in the bike lane for about two miles, then exited onto a shady driveway that sloped down a long hill to the lake. Dozens of people had also made the same decision for the day, and the grass around the lake was full of couples and families and pets lounging, playing, and even napping in the welcome spring sunshine.

After parking and locking their bicycles Holly and Abraham hiked to the top of a hill overlooking the lake. There were fewer people up there, so they spread a blanket from Abraham's pack in the shade of a tree and settled down for lunch.

"Are you hungry?" Abraham asked.

"I sure am!" Holly answered honestly.

"Nice," he chuckled. "Women won't always admit that." He removed chicken sandwiches with lettuce and sliced tomato, a plastic container full of grapes, another full of cheese cubes, and a bag of Chocolate chip cookies. She winced a little at his choice of wine, a sweet German white, but tried not to pass judgment—it might work with the foods he had packed. Inside the backpack were Velcro strips holding plates, cutlery, and wine glasses, and there were napkins that matched the blanket.

Holly smiled. "That's a very interesting backpack."

"Christmas present from my mother," he smiled back. "Glad to finally get a chance to use it. Shall I fill a plate for you, or would you prefer to help yourself?"

They ate companionably, watching the activity down by the lake and commenting on this and that. Neither was good at small talk. In the midst of one of the silences, Holly decided to open up about her conversation with Marcia, and she told Abraham about her plans to go to Pittsburgh.

"Funny: I kept thinking about that plate fragment. I agree that it could be something really interesting. I thought so as soon as I saw it, but when I held it in my hands, it felt like it had some kind of . . . ummmm . . . as if there were something special about it. Do you know anything more about it, either composition or provenance?"

Holly nodded. "There's more that I didn't tell you last night." She described how she had received the second piece, and she explained that another piece or pieces might still exist somewhere and that she might be able to find them.

"Wow. But, Holly, I get the sense that you've guessed something else that you're not telling me."

She smiled coyly. "I think it may be something worthy of a quest."

"A *quest*—interesting term. Keep me informed."

Silence again, but this time it was a silence full of anticipation and promise.

"And let me know if you can use an assistant: every now and then a historian is a good person to have around."

Their conversation paused again as they watched a little boy, who had been patiently waiting with his fishing pole for quite a while, finally get rewarded with a fish on his line. They agreed that it was immensely refreshing to see that some children still did things outdoors and didn't have their faces stuck to their smart phones or video games all day.

They cleaned up the lunch crumbs and took a walk around the lake, noting the deep indigo violets, the yellow buttercups, and the afternoon song of the birds assuring everyone that spring had arrived. Then they mounted their bicycles to return home. They took a turn around the park first, and as they rode for home, the sun began to set. It painted the sky first orange and bright blue, then brilliant red and navy blue, and then purple. The evening breeze was turning the air cool as they arrived at Holly's driveway.

They stepped away from the bicycles, and for a moment Holly wrestled with the idea of inviting him in. No, she thought, it's been a perfect day—perfect—and I don't want anything to spoil it.

"I'll call you before you leave for Pittsburgh," Abraham said quietly. Holy turned to face him squarely. She looked into his eyes and nodded slightly, having no idea of the effect that the fluttering of her lashes had on him. With no assurance that he was doing the right thing, Abraham slipped his arm around her and drew her close and kissed her.

I was wrong before, Holly thought as she melted into the kiss. *Now* it's been a perfect day. "I'll look forward to your call," she whispered. "Thank you for a wonderful day." Abraham smiled, then rode off as she waved to him from the driveway.

Holly went in and sat at her desk. Her thoughts went back and forth between her date with Abraham and the two plate fragments. She placed the pieces together, then took a pencil and paper and sketched what she could glean from the figures on the bottom. She imagined the third part that would complete the whole plate. She felt sure she had gotten the words right, but beyond that she could discern only some indistinct, slightly raised lines—not enough to determine a shape. But how about a *guess*. What if the dream of her father had given her a missing clue? *Graal*: could it mean a platter, a cup, a stone, or something else? The plate couldn't itself be the Grail: the material could be medieval, but no earlier, certainly not something from the turn of the Common Era. But it could be a serving platter, a less precious version of the one in the *Conte du Graal*. It could have held a Communion wafer: in Catholic belief the Body of Christ, not symbol, but presence. The plate, then, could be a Communion paten holding the body—and thus the mystery—of Christ. Thousands of such platters would have circulated in the Middle Ages, making this one valuable, worthy in its significance, but nothing rare or powerful in its own substance. But why would he show her the word in a book, and why would that word be the only word on the pages, unfolding one letter at a time?

Could the missing image on the bottom of the plate refer to a book? Did her father expect that she would know what book he meant, or did he intend that she should hunt for the book that unfolded the secret of the Grail? Would that book be one of the Grail Romances, or would it be a chronicle, something purporting to give the actual history of the Grail—not a story adapting religious themes to the adventures that noble medieval audiences loved so well?

Remember your Holmes, Holly thought: no reasoning without data. But where's the fun in that? Speculating about what the third piece of the plate might show would energize her whole week, and guessing some possible images would help her fill the time until her plane left. She wondered when Abraham would call, but decided she'd better not think too much about that if she wanted to get any work done. She looked at her "To Do" pad and remembered that she had to look for a rare volume of Icelandic sagas for a book collector and that she needed to pack, insure, and ship a couple pieces of heirloom jewelry. She also needed to make a couple hours' drive to negotiate with an antiques dealer over an early-American writing desk in which a client from California had expressed an interest, and she had several new arrowheads to clean, enter into her accounts, and place in the display.

Abraham called late on Wednesday apologizing that his work had kept him in the office late for a couple of nights. He was disappointed when Holly turned down his dinner invitation for Thursday, offering the excuse that she had a set of papers she absolutely had to finish grading.

"At least let me drive you to the airport Friday evening," Abraham offered.

"Thank you. I appreciate that very much."

"What time does your flight leave?"

"Five after seven: will that give you time after your last class?"

"I can pick you up a little before four o'clock. Should give us plenty of time."

"Great! See you then." She hesitated. "I'm looking forward to seeing you, Abraham."

She believed she could hear his smile. "Me, too. Good night, Holly."

"Good night." She listened for a moment as there was a pause before she heard the sound of the disconnection. Then she sighed and went back to work.

Friday afternoon arrived, and Holly threw the last of her personal items into her carry-on bag and printed out two copies of her e-ticket, placing one in her wallet and the other in her bag. She changed into comfortable travel clothes and began to think about how to ask the questions she needed to ask Marcia. Marcia was a friend, but she had no special experience with antiquities. Holly did not want Marcia to get the impression that she had given away something of great monetary value. She was nearly positive that the worth of the broken pieces of plate was not in their material cost, but in what they might lead to, and that was what she needed to determine.

Abraham arrived a few minutes early, dashingly preppy in his "business casual" khaki pants, boat shoes, and blue sweater over a white button-up shirt. As they headed to the airport, clouds rolled in soft and misty. They fell into a discussion about the deficiencies in the writing skills of most of their students, then laughed and decided not to waste their time together complaining. The airport roads and entryways were swarming, so Holly and Abraham were forced into a quick farewell. With a kiss, Abraham promised to be at the airport on Sunday evening promptly at eight to pick her up.

"Have fun, Holly. I can't wait to hear what you find out."

Holly felt strangely bereft as she watched him drive away. She clutched her travel bag and looked once more at her ticket, and her cell phone buzzed. She smiled at the text message: "Miss you already. A."

The long line for the security check was moving slowly, and Holly began to fear that she might miss her flight. When she finally got through, she decided to ignore the sweet, homey smell of the Cinnabon shop and hurried to her gate in time for the first call to board Flight 277 to Pittsburgh. Seeing another long, slow line, she realized the plane would be full, too. As she stood in line, she watched a story on the overhead television about the Greek government trying again to repatriate the Elgin Marbles from the British Museum.

Holly found her seat assignment and placed her carry-on bag in the bin above. She excused herself and pressed past a middle-aged woman and a girl of about ten to take her seat by the window. Looking out, she could see that the evening mist had begun to clear, and a few stars were emerging. The middle-aged woman was talking to the girl about her seat belt and when she could use the restroom and how the take-off would feel.

"Is this your first plane ride?" Holly asked the girl.

The girl smiled and nodded.

"Would you like to sit by the window? It's pretty cool to watch the lights down below. That is, if it's all right with you," she asked looking at the woman.

"What do you say?" the woman asked the girl.

"Thank you."

Holly moved to the aisle seat, pulled a mystery novel out of her purse, and made an effort to read, but visions of the possibilities that opened before her kept getting between her and the page. If only Marcia could lead her to some answers about the other piece of the plate . . .

The plane sat for some time on the tarmac, so it was nearly ten when they landed at Pittsburgh airport. Holly remembered that Marcia was a night owl, a good thing because she was not ready to settle in for the night and leave her questions until tomorrow. She texted Marcia that they were in and immediately received a reply that she was just coming in the main door. Holly was glad not to have to retrieve luggage at the carousel. She smiled at the woman and the girl, got her bag from the overhead bin, and stepped into another slow-moving line to deplane.

Marcia saw Holly first and came rushing to meet her. There was no way to mistake her even though her hair had turned mostly gray. Marcia had a fashion sense all her own. With her perfectly coiffed hair she wore tailored brown slacks and an animal print blouse, a heavy brown jacket, lots of gold jewelry (not the costume kind), and metallic gold pumps with four inch heels. Never were two friends more different, and Holly felt a little self-conscious in her khaki pants, red tunic, blue jean jacket and Sketchers.

"Hol! It's so good to see you! You never change. How long has it been?"

"Too long! You look great!"

"'Bout twenty pounds more of me than when we met last. Speaking of that, are you hungry? I know a great little coffee shop that's open all night."

"That sounds wonderful. I am a little hungry."

As much as Holly wanted to get straight to the point of her visit, she realized that she had to be patient— especially bad to be rude to an old friend. She followed Marcia out to her Honda Civic and listened to her friend's eager efforts to catch up on everything she had done since they'd last met. Holly smiled: Marcia never had needed a second party to have a conversation. As they maneuvered through the Friday night traffic of Pittsburgh's quirky streets, Marcia finally paused from her narrative to ask, "So what adventure brings you to Pittsburgh on such short notice?"

Holly laughed. "Why do you think there's an adventure?"

"C'mon Hol. Everything you do turns into some kind of adventure. Hey! What did you think of that artifact thing I sent you? Is it something interesting?"

Bingo! The very opening she was looking for.

"I think it is. Did you know that my father had a piece of the very same plate?"

"No kidding! Maybe that piece I sent is more important than I thought." Marcia turned into the parking lot of a hole-in-the-wall shop and lost her train of thought. They got out of the car, and Marcia led Holly inside. The coffee shop, almost a restaurant, had quaint but charming historical décor with plenty of atmosphere. A jazz combo of bass guitar, tenor sax, and upright piano played in one corner of the room. A fifty-ish woman with an Irish accent and a pleasant smile seated them at a small round table and left menus, promising to return in a moment. The menu featured long lists of beer and wine along with coffee and tea options, then crowded pages of upscale pub-food entrees alongside light appetizers and soups and salads.

"Oh, Marcia! This looks heavenly. Tell me what's best."

"Chicken salad on a croissant! The tuna is also brilliant! They have the best muffins in Pittsburgh. They're huge! And they make their own homemade brown sugar syrup for the coffees."

The woman returned. "What can I get for you now?" she asked.

Marcia ordered chicken salad on a croissant and an Irish coffee.

"I can't make up my mind," Holly said. "It all looks so wonderful. May I have the Pear and Arugula salad with a banana nut muffin—no, please make that a cranberry muffin with streusel topping—and a Murphy's Stout? Got to have an Irish beer in an Irish pub."

The food came quickly. Holly desperately wanted to get the conversation back to the missing piece of the plate, but she wasn't sure how, as Marcia was once again detailing one of her vacation trips to Europe.

"Now tell me everything," Marcia said, changing directions abruptly. "What have you been up to? Are you seeing anyone?"

The dreaded question, at least it always had been before. . . . Holly told her friend about Abraham, and as she spoke, she found herself wishing he were there sharing this *adventure*, as Marcia had called it.

"What about you?" she asked her friend. "How long has it been, five years since we flew to Buffalo for that wine auction?"'

"Yes. That was just before Dad got so sick. Losing him has been tough, Holly. I know you understand. We were both Daddy's girls, weren't we?"

"Yes, we were." They both got lost in their memories for a few moments. Marcia sipped her coffee and Holly her stout.

"Hey!" Marcia startled Holly out of her silence. "What about that piece of . . . whatever it was that I mailed to you? You started to tell me about it."

Holly dived in. "Marcia, you would be so amazed! I have another piece, one from Dad, of the *same plate*. The two parts fit together perfectly. That's one of the things I wanted to see you about. But there's at least one more missing piece. Do you have any idea what may have become of it?"

"Hmmmm . . . Yes, I do have an idea! Have you finished your drink? Come on, then!" Marcia grabbed her purse and the check, which she insisted on paying, and they headed back to the Honda and on to Marcia's apartment in Squirrel Hill.

When they arrived, Holly went to freshen up and settle into the guest room. If Holly's home was a museum of antiquities, Marcia's was a tribute to wardrobe accessories. There was a large closet in the guest room with shelves that housed dozens of pairs of shoes of all colors and designs, racks that held purses of different sizes and colors, something for every purpose, and hangers with jackets, kimonos, dusters, and scarves from the very formal to the very casual.

As Holly stood there with mouth open trying to figure out where to hang her own jacket, Marcia came in with a photo album. "This might hold your answer to the mystery of the missing piece."

Holly shrugged her jacket onto the bed as Marcia opened the cover of the album. There on the first page was a picture of her father in uniform, Marcia's father, also in uniform, and a woman who appeared to be a nurse. The caption under the picture was, "Les trois Mousquetaires."

As they turned the pages in the album, many pictures of the trio appeared, sometimes in uniform and sometimes in civilian clothing, either at the military base or in crowded cafés or at battered sites that looked like bombs had nearly leveled them.

"I would bet," Marcia said, "If there is a third piece, Colette would be the key. Maybe they found the plate together, and at the end of the war, each one took a piece as a memento."

"*Colette.* I do remember Father speaking the name once or twice. She was a nurse—the woman in the photo?"

"Yes, Colette Fourniere. Pop said they were very good friends."

"Did she come to America?"

"I don't believe she did. After Mom died, Pop talked about going to see her in Le Puy, but of course he never did."

"I wonder if she's still there. She'd have to be, what, over ninety years old?"

"Couldn't tell you, but the internet is a great thing. And by the way, I don't know why I remember this, but the name is spelled with an *e* at the end. Not *F, o u, r, n, i, e, r*, like *baker*, but *F, o, u, r, n, i, e, r, e*."

"Interesting."

"Would you like me to make a copy of this photo and send it to you?"

"I'd love that!"

"Two a.m." Macia yawned. "Well, I'm off to bed. Make yourself comfortable, and don't call me before eleven. This ol' girl's got to get her beauty sleep." Marcia gave her a hug. "I'm glad you're here, Hol. I've missed you."

"Thank you, Marcia. I've missed you, too. Good night." Holly wondered how Marcia could sleep after two coffees—must be the spike, she thought.

Holly kept her composure in front of her friend, but as soon as the bedroom door closed, she opened her travel bag and pulled out her laptop. It took about an hour, but Holly got an address and a phone number, same name, in Le Puy, France, the very town that marked the beginning of the major medieval Pilgrim route to Santiago de Compostela. As much as she would have loved to pursue it further, she felt a sudden exhaustion and quickly settled in for the night. She fell asleep with thoughts of France—food, wine, the Pilgrim Trail to Santiago, war memorabilia, and plate shards whirling in her head.

That night Holly dreamed of her father again. He was holding an ornate box in his hands. She came near to him, and he opened the box. Beams of light shot out in all directions, but she could not see what was in the box. He reached into the box and pulled out a candlestick that was burning with a steady flame. He greeted her in French, and then the dream dissolved away.

Something was making a buzzing noise. It was her cell phone. Holly picked it up. Nine o'clock. There were three text messages waiting for her, one from a client who was interested in purchasing an eighteenth century Spanish dining table, one from the airline informing her of a change in her flight number for the return, and one from Abraham. She opened the one from Abraham even though her eyes were not quite clear yet.

"Enjoy your day. See you tomorrow at 8."

"Abraham," Holly spoke to her phone, "how's your French?" She smiled and walked out to the kitchen where she started a pot of coffee. While she waited for it, she perused Marcia's impressive wine collection. That was one thing they had always shared, a love of fine wines.

Marcia shuffled down the hall in a pink robe and fuzzy slippers about thirty minutes later. "Don't you want to move in with me so you can fix the coffee every morning?" she asked Holly.

Holly grinned. "Maybe you just need to marry a barista."

"Oh no. Date one, maybe, but I don't intend to go down that other road again. Once was pul-en-ty."

Holly laughed. "What are our plans for today?"

Marcia opened up a box and offered it to Holly. "Breakfast."

"Blueberry scones! You remembered!"

"Of course: I wouldn't forget your favorite. There are some new exhibits at the Westmorland Museum of Art, and it's a good time of year for the botanical gardens. Either one of those interest you?"

"Both."

"It's both then."

They clinked their coffee cups in a toast to the day, and as soon as they finished their scones and coffee, they dressed to leave.

The women spent a very companionable day walking the halls of the museum and the aisles full of budding plants, did a little accessory shopping at some of Marcia's favorite boutiques, and then went for dinner. After cashew crusted tilapia with Jamaican rum butter and sweet potato couscous accompanied by a bottle of Pascal Jolivet Sancerre, they drove back to Marcia's house and took a short walk around Squirrel Hill. Holly's mind kept going back to an exhibit of ornamental boxes at the Museum: they brought back to mind the dream from the night before.

"Holly, this has been a real treat. Promise me you'll stay in touch. I really miss having you around. Since Pop's been gone, it's been kind of hard to fill the void."

"I understand. It's been hard for me, too. I wish we lived closer."

"Promise to keep me up-to-date with the artifact things, too—and about Abraham, of course! Let me know if you find Colette. I'm tempted to say let's catch a plane together and just fly over and look around, but I don't think I can get off work with so little notice."

Holly promised.

"So you think you may have something serious with this Abraham, or just a fling?" Marcia winked.

They spent the rest of their time recalling past adventures and looking through photo albums. As they prepared to go to the airport, Marcia brought a wrapped box to Holly.

"What's this?"

"Open it."

Holly carefully unwrapped the present. It was a framed photograph of Holly at about age seven standing next to her father, holding his hand. She couldn't hold back the tears. "Thank you so much," she whispered. "I'll treasure it."

"Let's get you home," Marcia said, "and don't forget that promise!" They hugged each other. "What is it with friends these days?" Marcia asked. "You hardly ever see the old ones, and new ones seem impossible to find."

The skies remained clear, and Holly's flight home left and arrived on time. Abraham stood waiting for her at the end of the terminal.

"Well?" he asked, offering to carry her travel bag. "Find any new treasures in Pittsburgh?"

"Information," Holly answered, smiling. "The next step in the quest for . . ."

"For what?"

"I'm not telling yet."

"Not telling!"

"No."

Abraham laughed aloud. "So you're leaving me with an even bigger mystery than the one you're trying to solve."

"Yes."

"All right. I won't press. But I hope you'll tell me about it when you feel ready."

"Oh, I will. I may even need your advice to solve it."

"My advice? Why?"

"You may have a piece of the puzzle, too, without even knowing it."

"That's got to make me a little more appealing as a companion. The weather looks good for the drive home—we've been lucky lately. As soon as you get away from the airport, the sky's really clear and bright—I think it's a blue moon tonight."

"Have you ever studied the Santiago de Compostela Pilgrim Trail?" Holly asked.

"Hmmm, no—I do mostly Modern Europe—but a few years ago an English medievalist friend of mine walked all the way from Le Puy to Santiago. Amazing experience he said, and the Cathedral in Santiago is really something—I've seen his pictures. Why did you ask?"

"Something I need to know more about."

"I can put you in touch with my friend if you'd like, but if you're interested in something about contemporary France, I can probably help you myself."

"Lovely. I suspect I'll take you up on that offer."

They got back to town too late to go out, so Abraham dropped Holly at home.

"You've been a dear, playing chauffeur," she said. "I owe you dinner. Maybe next weekend?"

"Might be two weeks: I have two batches of exams coming in this week and may need the whole weekend to finish them. But dinner will give me something to look forward to when I've finished them."

Over the next few days Holly sent a thank-you card to Marcia with some antique lace from a local shop, caught up on her work, and then thought about how best to contact Colette Fourniere. Trying to call someone from another country whom you've never met may seem too forward, she thought. She hadn't located an email. "Letter," she said aloud to herself: slow, but probably the best method. While her reading skill was still pretty good, she'd fallen out of practice with conversational French, so after spending a few days with her old Rosetta Stone cd's, she decided to write the note first in English and then translate it.

How to word it? Something like this: first, give her name and credentials; second, seeking information about Colette Fourniere, a military nurse and friend of my father and Harold Joseph, two American soldiers, during the Second World War; third, include a copy of the photo that Marcia had sent with the "Three Musketeers"; fourth, "can you please help me"—best to be brief, friendly, informative, but not insistent or intrusive. She finished the letter, kissed the envelope for luck, and put it in the mail the next day.

A couple weeks later Holly and Abraham had dinner together at the only Italian restaurant in town, fortunately a very good family place with an excellent wine list. Holly insisted that she pick up the bill as thanks for his taking her to and from the airport, and at liberty to spend as she wished, she ordered a big Barolo for them to drink with dinner—it went perfectly with her eggplant parmigiana and grilled vegetables and his linguini with steak Gorgonzola.

"How's your quest going?" Abraham asked, as they both swirled the wine in their glasses and compared their impressions of aroma and taste.

"Right now I'm just waiting," Holly said. "I sent an inquiry to someone in Le Puy, and I need to get a response before I can take the next step."

"Oh, Le Puy: is that why you asked about the Pilgrim Trail?"

"Yes, partly."

"Funny thing. My mother came from there."

"Your mother? What was her name?"

"Celestine. Her maiden name was Fourniere."

"Now that's just spooky."

"Why?" he laughed.

"Because I sent a letter to a woman named Colette Fourniere."

"You did! Imagine that. That was my aunt's name, my mother's sister."

"Was?"

"Yes. She passed away just a couple years ago."

"Then my letter will never reach her."

"No, but it may reach her daughter, my cousin. She has the same name: Colette Fourniere, or had it until she got married and took her husband's name. But I'm sure a number of people still know her by her maiden name."

"She's named for her mother—interesting. Alive and well?"

"Last I knew. She's just about our age."

"Do you stay in touch?"

"Christmas cards, and every now and then I call to wish her well and find out about the family. Would you like me to call her for you?"

Holly put down her wine glass so she wouldn't spill it. The room was beginning to spin, and not from the wine. "Well, yes, of course!"

"But then you'll have to tell me a little more about your mystery so that I'll know what to ask her when we talk."

"I guess I should. How's your French?"

"*Comme ci, comme ça*—I can manage in a pinch, and Colette speaks a little English, too, so we have a pretty good conversation when I call."

"Tell me about Colette."

She grew up in Le Puy and lives there now with her husband. She studied nursing like her mother, and then almost entered a convent, but she met René and fell in love and got married. Now she does some work in artistic textiles—used to work part-time at a wine shop. They have two really nice children: one is a musician, and one finished college a couple years back. You may even have met her: she spent a semester here at the College through the study-abroad program. Her name is Renae Thibeau."

"Abraham, what are your plans after the semester ends?"

"None right now, beyond getting back to work on an article about the restoration of French churches after the war—got to finish it over the summer. You have something in mind?"

"Depending on the reply to my letter or your phone call, I may be pursuing my quest to the town of Le Puy, France, and I wouldn't mind the assistance of a Modern European History Professor who speaks good French."

"Will it be dangerous?"

"I hope so."

"Then count me in."

"Lovely. We should leave as soon as we can to beat the high tourist season."

"Right. Here's another idea, if you don't mind my intruding on your plans. Why not ask your friend Marcia if she can go along. Doesn't she have a stake in your adventure, too?"

"Very thoughtful of you, and an excellent idea. She may not be able to go—I don't know if she can get the time off work—but I should ask anyway. What fun! Oh, if you can speak with Colette Fourniere, here's what I need to know. Remember that plate fragment I showed you? Marcia sent me the second piece. And I think Colette Fourniere, Senior, may have known about the third fragment."

"How about that now . . . I'll call my cousin early tomorrow afternoon—that should be evening her time. If her mother had anything like that, Colette will probably know about it: she's an only child and inherited everything of her mother's. Question is whether she'd have kept it. Only one way to find out. Say, this Barolo is really extraordinary, but you shouldn't have spent so much money on me."

"I spent it on me, too," Holly said, sipping happily.

Late Monday evening Abraham called.

"Sorry I didn't get right back to you, Holly. I called Colette on Sunday, but didn't reach her right away. I left a message, and she called back this morning. Said she'd love to have us visit. Their flat is plenty big, which is unusual there, or she can arrange lodging with a friend a few doors down who has a B&B—rooms available, if we get there before high tourist season begins. Three rooms either free or *at family rates*, if Marcia can come along."

"How soon can you leave after term ends?"

"I'll need a couple days to get grades done and in, but by no later than Wednesday after graduation."

"I'll call Marcia tomorrow to see if we need two tickets or three."

"Probably Pittsburgh to New York to Paris."

"Are you up for secretarial duty?" Holly asked.

"Absolutely. Any further information on the mystery?"

"I'm hoping we'll find what we need to solve it in Le Puy."

"Colette said she has a bunch of items that her mother left: mostly arts, crafts, and pop memorabilia, but also a few much older artifacts, some Classical and Renaissance, but some medieval. We're welcome to look through all of them."

"Can you ask ahead about that third piece from the plate?"

"Certainly," Abraham replied. "I'll mention it next time I call. Weather's supposed to be nice next weekend— maybe I can catch you up over lunch and a walk?"

"Lovely."

Next evening Holly called Marcia—after getting an email from Abraham that Colette had found some odd, broken bits in her mother's collection.

"Wow," Marcia said, "you really know how to live up to your promises. What's on your mind?"

"Lots, but I'll get right to the main part: would you have any interest in a trip to France—Le Puy, specifically?"

"When?"

"Right after our semester ends, just around the middle of May—can you get off work then?"

"I've been itching for a vacation, and that sounds perfect. I've always wanted to visit some of the places Pop saw, you know, during the War. So count me in—I just have to check airline prices."

"Flight's on me: got a bunch of travel miles with my new credit card. And we've found some really good lodgings, so all you're in for is train fare and food."

"And wine."

"Of course."

"You said we: it won't be just the two of us?"

"Three of us: Abraham's joining us."

"Oh, Hol, I don't want to be a third wheel."

"Asking you along was Abraham's idea, and you won't be a third wheel. Well, I guess each of us will be an equal wheel. He has a cousin—believe this—in Le Puy, and there's a chance she may have the third piece to the plate. It will be like the Three Musketeers all over again."

"Unbelievable—I can't wait!"

On the Ides of May Holly and Abraham flew together to New York, where they met Marcia, who had joined them from Pittsburgh. They took an overnight, uneventful flight to Paris. Holly fell asleep with her cheek propped against a bulkhead, and she had a vivid dream. She was a child again, and she was looking up at a cup that stood on top of the mantel, over the fireplace. For no apparent reason, the cup fell off and shattered at her feet. She felt terrified. Then she looked back up on the mantel. A green stone about the size of her fist stood where the cup had been. It, too, fell off and broke into pieces. She began to cry, wondering what to do. She turned toward the center of the room, and there stood her father, looking at her. "Daddy," she said, I think I broke 'em." "No you didn't, dearest," he said. "Don't worry. They can't be broken." He knelt down and scooped up the broken shards in his hands. "Watch," he said. He took them over to a lamp stand, where a small, leather-bound book lay open. He dropped the shards into the book, the closed the two sides, and the book seemed to have swallowed them. He picked up the book, which had begun to glow with a low, green light. "See?" he said. "That's my girl." Holly woke, and the dream seemed as clear to her as if it had happened in real life.

That night they checked into a hotel near the Gare de Lyon, agreeing to meet for an early lunch.

Holly and Abraham met at a little before eleven and found a table at the charming bistro just a block from the hotel. They ordered bread and cheese and wine and waited for Marcia to arrive. They heard the sound of clicking heels before they saw Marcia round the corner, bags on her arms, sequined scarf blowing in the breeze. "I found the most darling shoes!" She announced and bounced into a chair beside them.

"I don't know if I'm more amazed that you already found a place to shop or that you got up early enough to do it!" Holly laughed.

"Nothing like French fashion," Marcia winked.

"And French wine," Abraham added.

"And perfect company," Holly concluded. They raised their glasses as the waiter arrived. After lunch, they left by train for the next destination in their quest.

Early in the evening the trio reached Le Puy, the traditional beginning of the Santiago de Compostela Pilgrim Trail. Abraham had got directions to his cousin's flat. She and her husband owned the top story of an older stone building up a steep side street only a few blocks from the train station. Slowed down a little by Marcia's new shoes, the travelers eventually arrived at Colette's building and rang up the apartment.

A voice responded from the intercom at the door as soon as they buzzed. "*Alors! Bienvenu!*" And in a few seconds a woman, slim and refined looking, about the same age as her three visitors, opened the door.

"Abraham! It has been too long since you visited!" She spoke heavily accented but clear English in gravelly alto tones. They kissed each other on both cheeks, and Abraham immediately introduced Colette Fourniere Thibeau to Holly and Marcia. "I am so happy you have come. Please feel welcome. René will be so glad to meet you, too. We must climb some stairs, but the flat is so lovely—worth every step. You will see. The girls will be sorry they missed you: Renae has graduated and is working in the states, in New York, and Nicolette will not be home from university for a few more days—unless of course you can stay that long? You will stay with us, of course, since we have the rooms."

René, of medium height but with a broad chest and a square jaw, met them at the top of the stairs, shaking hands and taking their bags off to the guest rooms. He spoke jovially with Abraham in French, and Holly and Marcia joined in tentatively, gaining confidence as they realized they could at least make themselves understood.

"I haven't spoken any French since college," Marcia whispered to Holly.

"From what I can tell," Holly whispered back, "you're doing wonderfully!"

The flat was indeed astonishingly large, open concept with a grand foyer and pillared transitions to a dining room, sitting room, and kitchen, and double glass doors that led to a patio overlooking a courtyard, but with views of the town over adjoining roofs. The guest rooms, comfortable and well appointed, felt airy, with the windows open to welcome a gentle breeze.

By the time they got back to the sitting room, Colette had opened a cool Pouilly-Fumé, and René was just bringing in a tray of hors d'oeuvres, followed by a buffet dinner of pike, local meats and vegetables, and an apple tart, with a lightly sweet Sauterne for a *digestif*. Later Colette brought out a large box of carefully wrapped objects.

"Holly, I did my best to sort through my mother's artifacts, and these seemed to most likely to fit your search. I put in a few other pieces simply because I thought they may interest you."

"Thank you: that's very generous," Holly said, and they all sat down to go through the pieces together.

After only a few minutes, Holly found what she was looking for.

"I think this is it. Would you excuse me for a moment, please?" Doing her best to keep calm, Holly went to her room and drew out the two other plate fragments, then returned to the others.

"Let's be sure." She laid her two pieces together on a table, then placed the third as well.

It fit nearly perfectly.

"Amazing," Abraham said.

Then Holly carefully turned it over to show the bottom of the plate. It showed three shapes, each worn by time and use, but still distinguishable.

"The one in the middle looks like a thin booklet," Marcia said.

"And this one," Abraham said, "may be a candlestick in a holder?"

"And this one a paten, I think, to hold the Host," Holly said.

The inscription on the side of the plate lay completely visible as well.

"Colette," Marcia said, "I'd like to show you something. She took from her purse the photo she had shown Holly of the Three Musketeers: her father, Holly's father, and Colette's mother.

"*Incroyable*," Colette muttered. "I have one just like it! *Pardonnez-moi*." She hurried off and returned a moment later with what looked like the same picture in a small frame. "Mmm, I think I remember something." She took the photo out of the frame and handed it to Marcia.

"Not exactly the same, but pretty much," Marcia said, looking carefully at the details.

"What's that on the back of your photo, Marcia?" Holly asked. "Looks like someone wrote something there. Very faint . . ."

"Rocamadour 1946," Abraham said. "Look: you can just read an inscription under the lamplight."

"I could barely see that before," Marcia said. "It just looked like scratches to me."

"Yes, that's in front of the Basilique St. Sauveur in Rocamadour, along the Pilgrim Way," Colette said. "I recognize it. Not the famous church with the Black Madonna, Chapelle Notre Dame, but the other, just as interesting. Mother took me there once. But look at this photo. She gave me this one when I was very young and told me always to keep it. She said that one day I should go there with some very good friends, and I might just find something quite important."

"What were you supposed to find?" Marcia asked.

"Ah, I have no idea. She never told me."

"Marcia examined the second photograph more carefully. "The background doesn't look exactly the same." René asked to look at it.

"*Doc, il est non le même place. C'est le Cathédral Notre-Dame du Puy—ici, dans Le Puy, sur le Roche Corneille.*

"Yes, Colette said," they held the same pose for the photo, but the background is different because they took it in a different place. My mother was born in Rocamadour, but she came here to live in Le Puy after the war—maybe this was the last picture the three of them took together."

"Can you see anything on the back of the second photo?" Abraham asked.

Marcia turned it over. "Three triangles, each with one slightly rounded edge."

"Can we visit this cathedral?" Holly asked.

"*Certainement,*" René answered, "*nous* ... climb up .. . *dans le matin?*" He made a motion with his fingers of climbing up steps.

"It's the highest point in Le Puy," Colette explained. "But not too hard for people on a quest."

"Exciting," Holly said. "I think we are getting very near."

Holly woke in the middle of the night with light from a three-quarters moon shining in her window. A dream image remained clear in her mind. She was standing with other people beneath a window with light streaming down. Three people, a woman and two men, stood in front, next to a stone altar, with their backs to her. The man in the middle turned around and looked at her. He was smiling. It was her father. He moved a little to the side, motioning to an object sitting on the altar: a plate about a foot in diameter with a book placed on top of it. Behind the plate and book stood a candle that burned brightly. He nodded to Holly and held both hands out toward her as if she were to take them in her own. As she moved toward him, the dream ended, and she woke.

In the morning Colette laid out croissants, both hot and iced coffee, fresh fruits, and hard-cooked eggs. The Americans had all brought clothing for hiking, and they dressed comfortably for an outing. Marcia, of course, raised the fashion bar for hiking. Her leather, ankle-high boots were purple and the socks that showed just above them were the same purple. Khaki shorts and blouse, starched and pressed over a purple cheetah print tank top with a purple belt were completed by a safari hat wrapped in a purple scarf. She turned slowly and allowed everyone too *Oooooo* and *Ahhhhh* over the ensemble.

"*Tres bon,*" Colette said, "but everyone will need comfortable shoes. We have a few kilometers to hike, and much of it is uphill, so we will need most of the day to walk there and back and to explore."

A town of white and brown stone buildings with orange roofs, Le Puy nestled among rolling hills with its cathedral sitting singularly atop a steep hill filled with vibrant life. The day was warm, but a refreshing breeze made it a perfect day for their adventure. After strolling through many streets, following René's lead, they finally began their climb to the top. Finding the Roche Corneille presented no problem, since they could see it from nearly anywhere in town, but they took a little time exploring before trudging up the steep hill and climbing the final set of stairs to the cathedral entrance.

The stolid brown façade of the cathedral displayed three sections each with rounded arches and a tall doorway. "Three doors, three triangles, and three friends from the photos," Marcia announced, proud of her discovery.

The Romanesque interior had a slim nave decorated with some very old frescoes, a number of statues, and, as in Rocamadour, a black Madonna, in this case with a child as well. It was tempting to spend hours just admiring the cathedral itself, but the group felt eager to pursue their goal.

"Now for the final task," Holly spoke quietly. "Let's solve this mystery." They split up and each searched in different directions keeping in mind a candle, a paten and a book. After a few moments, something in a simple side chapel along the nave caught Holly's eye.

A niche in the stone with a rectangular stand in the middle—on top of the stand sat a round, gray plate, on top of the plate sat a thin, leather-bound booklet, and behind both stood a lighted candle.

Along the side of the plate, Holly could just read the words *via, veritas, vita*. On top of the book she thought she could discern the incision of a simple drawing: three hands clasped together, and around them lines pointing in all directions, as if to indicate that the hands were emitting light.

"Look," Holly called to the others. I think we've found another clue."

"What is it?" Marcia asked.

"I have an idea," Holly said. "I think Colette's mother wanted us to come here. She wanted us to find this together."

"Find what?" Colette asked.

"The Holy Grail!" Holly answered.

"The Holy Grail?" Abraham was stunned.

"She knew where to find the cup of Christ?" Colette was astonished.

"Maybe not a cup at all," Holly said. "I wonder if we're looking at it right there."

"I'm confused," Marcia said. "It's not a cup?"

"Here's an odd thing about that legend," Abraham said, nodding. "When the word *grail* or *graal* first appeared in the Middle Ages, it didn't refer to the cup of Christ—that idea came later. The word occurred in southern France and northern Spain, a contraction of *gradual*, and it referred to the Lenten prayer missal, a book which gradually unfolded the 'secrets' of Christ leading up to Easter: the Crucifixion, the Resurrection, and later, the Assumption."

"So the Holy Grail," Marcia mused, "isn't a cup at all, but a booklet with a record of the masses leading up to Easter Sunday, an unfolding of the mysteries of Christ."

"*Mon Dieu,*" René whispered, "*il est ici!*"

"Yes. But I'd never heard that till now," Holly said, "That answers a lot of questions and helps interpret some strange and wonderful dreams. It also shows me something else of great value."

"What's that?" Abraham asked.

"For one thing, having a traveling secretary with a PhD in history is a great asset. But you do Modern history, not medieval. How did you know that about the grail?"

"A little hobby of mine back in graduate school. One summer I did a bunch of research on the legends and iconography of holy objects. It was fun, but I never thought anything practical would come of it. But speaking of practical, what do we do now?"

"We need to check to see if that small book is indeed the Lenten missal," Holly said.

"And if we've really found it?" Marcia asked. "What should we do? It looks as though no one's given that poor little book much notice."

"I know the answer to that," Colette said. "We pray together, to thank God for what we've seen and for the company with whom we've seen it, to show the grail the respect it deserves."

Holly looked around. She knew she should ask someone first, but if they were going to get an expert to show her the book, they would call in someone just like her, an expert in working with antiquities, so she pulled a pair of cotton gloves out of her pocket, put them on, gingerly picked up the little book, and opened it. With eyes shining, she turned around and held it out for all her companions to see.

With effulgent hearts, they all knelt together beside the niche as the last golden afternoon light dropped through a window on the opposite wall like a banderole.

"The Three Musketeers have become five," Marcia whispered to Holly.

"And when we tell others our story, we'll become many more. This treasure was not meant to be a secret, hidden away in a niche. It should bring joy to everyone." Holly answered. "*Kyrie eleison,*" she chanted softly in her resonant alto.

"*Christe eleison,*" the others responded in unison.

A WALK IN THE DARK

Marie de France
Dreams of Steampunk

(appeared in The Journal of
Contemporary Rhetoric, Fall 2017)

FFFFSST! THE WICK OF THE BEESWAX CANDLE FUSSED TO life as she touched to it the spill she had lit at the fire in the hearth.

Marie could not sleep. She had got up and padded from her bed across the cold floor to the window that looked out over the keep—she could hear from the other side of Dover Castle the sound of the surf hustling, furling, whirling, and withdrawing again.

She could see the darkness gathering itself like a hood, the stars like a thousand eyes beaming from underneath. She had gone from the window to the mantel of the great stone hearth for the solace of candlelight.

But something else was cuddling up to her thoughts and purring with a hum like a hive of working bees, something loud and insistent enough that even after a deep draught of fresh air and a lingering look at the crescent moon in the clear night sky she could not return to her pillow.

A shadow, dark and metallic, surrounded her, embraced her like a wave, and fled, rumbling, leaving her behind.

She felt as if Bisclavret had called her from sleep and cried, "Marie, bring my clothes, please, for my wife has left me cold and hungry in the woods, and I would not travel among noble folk in nothing but a grey pelt, however fine!"

Not a real sound wringing the sensual ear, but a spirit from the world of dreams, some rough beast waiting to be born . . . Not a wolf, not a vampire, not a Christmas ghost, but another voice had called her firmly, irresistibly out of sleep. It called each time she wafted from twilight toward dreams; it called with the voice of the owl—or the call of the kettle on the fire, or the mad flash of the bolt from the arbalest as it pierces the pillar-posted targe and another's already pulled quick from the quiver. It was a practical sound, not an artful one, a guildsman's mechanical sound, not the virtuous marksmanship of a yeoman or a knight or of a lady in playful contest.

She did not recognize the sound—she could have said "*like* this," but could not have said, "Aye, *oui*, it *is* this."

Henry II loved holidays there at the castle only a day's ride from Canterbury, and he had summoned Marie to tell his favorite story, "Lanval," after the afternoon banquet. No matter how many times she had told the lai in his presence, he never shied from requesting it again and clapping thunderously with an enormous smile crossing his face like a burst of sunshine when she had finished. Dover Castle had become his particular favorite, a renovation project, and he had called court there for Christmas to inaugurate its nearly completed refurbishment. Of course such an occasion once again demanded his favorite story, the tale of a fine but poor knight rescued from Gwenevere and Arthur by his beautiful beloved faerie princess.

"The resurrection of a castle to celebrate the birth of the Christ-child," Henry had said with another of those beaming smiles and a booming laugh, shaking his red-brown mane like a proud lion. "And the resurrection of a condemned man though love and the magic of Avalanna!"

Henry enjoyed King Arthur stories. He especially liked stories of troublesome women who found themselves silenced by their own folly or by the wisdom of men. But he also loved stories of men and women who crossed boundaries beautiful or bitter into magical lands beyond place and time and of the adventures they had there. "The magic of story is a gift from God," he had often said.

Marie liked the Arthurian tales, too, but she preferred stories of bright and able women who either had or found a way to gain control of their own situations—and Christian stories of course.

She threw a long cloak around her shoulders over her night dress, but let her hair fall free to her shoulders. Night hours away from the convent and free of the habit felt heavenly.

Marie stood still for a moment holding her candle aloft to find her ways to the stairs. She thought she heard a bell clang: once, twice, three times. Its eager clang rose and fell, rose and fell, rose and fell as it echoed through the banquet hall below. It seemed to her more a dull summons than a shriek of fear in the night.

But, no, she had heard no bell. It may have been a phantom, a nervous memory of the habitual calls to prayer on the canonical hours. It may have been something deep below her waking thoughts warning her to go no farther.

As she reached the head of the stairs, faint smells of roast lamb, of braised beef and root soup and pease porridge with herbs, fresh bread brushed with warmed butter wafted up the cascade of steps—does one smell things in dreams?

Yes, she couldn't have heard that sound: she heard no rustling and rushing of anyone else rising from sleep and dashing toward the call of warning or command. The sound had come, like the feeling and the image, from the realm of sleep.

But the smells were real, as real as they steep staircase where she stood, prepared to step down in as near as she could to silence.

Before she descended, she let her thought take fuller shape.

She had first dreamed of "Equitan," the story that always troubled her so much. Many Religious often asked her for that one: a knight with a beautiful wife falls for a more beautiful damsel; the wife grants him release from the marriage so that he may have the damsel and becomes a nun; when the knight and his new wife grow older and tired, they release each other and, well-taught by the first wife, they too retire from the world to end their days in contemplative prayer far from the passions of this transitory life. Her listeners could seldom just let a story be a story. Marie wondered if they saw the allegory as she did, or if they (monks) simply loved to approve of the husband's decision, or if they (nuns) loved to disapprove of the husband and cling to the first wife, or if they (priests) loved to see the progress from sin and attachment to redemption and hermetic prayer.

But Equitan and his loves had passed away in the gossamer of an early-night dream. Another, a fragment, had taken its place, one from the flood-tide of midnight, when dreams take fuller shape and substance in the present, in sense and the pulse of blood rather than in old stories.

Equitan, character and tale, had given way to physical presence, to the heft, the weave, the smell, to the artful, motive, liveliness of the tapestries, the flowing wall-hangings that sat opposite the great leaping and pounding fire of the cavernous banquet-hall of Dover Castle below her. The tapestries—no, *one* of them—summoned her no less insistently than the confessor, the king, or the death-bell.

Henry's improvements to the castle had included not just repairs and structural additions, but also decoration. He had tapestries brought from Firenze and Madrid, and had commissioned French and Flemish weavers for specific designs, and one he had had made in Winchester by his own English craftsmen, the best he could find among the folk he ruled. One of the English master-weavers he had called a mad genius, equally worthy of praise and pensions as of cell safe from the potential to influence Normans or Saxons alike. His figures, Henry said, seemed to come to life before one's eyes, almost to move and speak.

That one had caught Marie's eye, and it had already invaded and placed its banner in her dreams, increasing her pulse and flushing her skin even in sleep.

She remembered a large dun-colored background with three levels: they swept from left to right, turning at the right edge of the tapestry and rising to the second level, then turning again at the left edge and rising again to a conclusion on the right.

At the bottom left stood the figure of a man driving an ox-cart. Whereas most woven figures, except perhaps for churchmen, kings, and of course Christ, looked much the same, this one seemed to take life as one looked at it. It held to the proportions of a man, and it seemed almost sentient, ready to drive its cart up the road ahead.

Marie felt as though she must, must have another look at that tapestry. It drew her like first light to lauds or consecration to the Eucharist—she could hardly shape such thoughts in the privacy of her own mind.

She took a deep breath, smiled—she admitted that a holiday away from the convent, a few short days with family and old friends in a fine castle, telling stories and laughing—felt good, very good indeed, and holding her candle above and before her began carefully, trembling, to descend the long, stone staircase. Her heart galloped as if it would run on ahead of her. She resolved to pray for forgiveness later.

She saw lying by the fire the body of man stretched out among a mound of rough blankets: Arnolf, the man who tended the fires and kept the castle stocked with wood and kindling. He had drunk his share and more of ale after his evening's duties—Henry always permitted him to listen to the storytelling, since he knew how much the servant loved them—and he slept deeply and innocently, not even snoring. He would not wake until morning unless Marie woke him.

The fire in the great hearth still popped and rumbled, tossing flames high and sharp like cathedral spires. Its light spread alternating sunbursts and shadows across the high, broad hall, turning darkened corners into bright morning and high-backed chairs into contorted phantoms. Tall and slim, Marie cast, as she stepped slowly downward, a shadow that stretched and sharpened like the last fingers of daylight, pushing day into waiting dusk.

As she reached the banquet floor, the leonine fire echoed in a quick burst, yet the sound seemed to Marie more a welcome than a warning: it faded into crackles of laughter.

Hastening, she bumped a stray chair and nearly knocked it over, but she caught it with her free hand and set it upright without thinking—her eyes and her thoughts had already locked on the tapestries opposite the fire.

The first, on her left as she turned to face the wall fully, showed the figure of a Florentine maid embracing the neck of a unicorn amidst a lush wood—a favorite device of the Continental tapestries, she knew, which were just beginning to get interesting. The maiden seemed to her surprisingly expressionless, while the unicorn looked quite content with her caresses—obviously the design of a man without consultation with a woman.

The next, from Madrid, showed a boy and a girl playing with a dog, dancing or leaping through what looked like a vegetable garden. The three looked as happy as they could be, and the word *May* appeared above them to show that they were enjoying the coming of Spring. As lively and colorful as was the field of vision, the weaver had not entirely succeeded with the figures: while the colors rose easily to life, the proportions and expressions looked static, the angles not quite correct, the oblong faces almost ghoulish—no one would have dared to say a word about it to Henry, who was fond of its playfulness.

The third tapestry, Parisian, showed a roadway going toward a town. Along it peasants worked in a field, mended fences, and washed clothes in a stream, but at its end the road moved into a town overflowing with guildsmen who were completing the town's wall and drawing in carts full of building materials.

The fourth tapestry she examined came from Flanders, but it had been made for Norman lords. It had two parts, side by side: scenes from the life of the blessed Christ, speaking the Beatitudes from the mount, turning water into wine, sharing a final supper with his Disciples; Norman soldiers celebrating victory on the battle ground of Hastings. The Christian scenes came to life for her, partly because they had shaped so much of her own life; the battle scenes stirred at once a sense of horror and a twinge of pride.

Then, finally, Marie turned to the largest tapestry of all of them, the one that Henry had brought from Winchester. It stood nearest the corner and rose to nearly twice the height of the others, and the fire from the great hearth cast light and shadow over the scene as it unfolded in three rising tiers.

Once she had seen it, this tapestry would not let go of her imagination.

It had brought her from sleep to the flickering light of the banquet room to see for herself its magic.

Its narrative rose in boustrophedon fashion from left to right, and began with a young man beside an ox-cart that had begun laboring its way up a path that curled along a hillside. The man looked directly at the viewer and pointed in the direction the ox-cart was heading. He had a hint of a smile on his clean-shaven face. He wore a shirt and trousers rather than hose and a tunic, and he had a piece of cloth around his neck, perhaps to shield his skin from the sun.

The eye following the direction in which he pointed would see a lively world unfolding scene by scene as the rode rose up the hill. Pursuing quickly one would see, on the first level with the carter, laborers of all sorts, and farmers taking their wares to market, kicking up clouds of dust; on the second level monks and nuns, palmers, traveled, some as if on pilgrimage, some returning home, and craftsmen of all sorts strode ahead to barns and shops with their arms laden with tools and materials and drawings—they faced both eager customers and dubious merchants to hawk their wares; again the narrative turned back, and on the third level, leading at the top to a small castle with a church and a keep, knights and ladies sat on a lawn singing to the accompaniment of musical instruments, a lyre, a shawm, and a small drum, while an open field stood prepared for a tournament, and tables, spread for a banquet, awaited the hungry participants. Near the very top, ambassadors had come from a far land to dine with the lord and lady of the castle: they looked out from a high window in the keep and waved hello to the newcoming visitors.

She heard a low sound like pleasant laughter.

The young man's hair looked tousled, as though a breeze had blown it.

"Listen," said and voice. "And watch."

The young man's mouth had moved. Marie was sure of it.

His face had turned. He was looking ahead, in the direction of the ox-cart's movement, and again he was laughing, a pleasant, tinkling sound. Marie's eyes followed his glance. The ox's legs struggled to life to pull the cart, and the ox let out a snort. She returned her eyes to the young man, and his whole arm, extended to full length, now pointed to Marie's right, ahead in his narrative. Again she heard a sound of laughter, and she could still see, even in profile, a broad smile on his face. Again she let her eyes move to the right.

From the stillness of tightly woven fibers, the tapestry was coming to life before her eyes, and it made her spine tingle and her skin run cold. A tear came to her eye, one such as a sudden fear will bring, but she could not take her gaze from the scene on the wall, as it creaked and groaned into sense and activity.

How could dead fibers move? And how could they laugh? Was she seeing witchcraft, or just the deceiving shadows of the leaping tongues of fire, or a truer magic, that of the artisan artist whose creation stepped through the plane of creation into time and space beyond?

Did her stories do that, Marie wondered?

But the tapestry images were certainly moving! It jerked her out of thought and out of self-consciousness into its story, into its people.

The ox on the young man's cart grunted, and his feet shuffled back clouds of dust as the cart surged up the road. "Hi!" the man yelled to encourage the beast on its way. The cart wavered for an instant, and then pulled ahead up the road.

The dust rolled on in a wave that for an instant obscured two fence menders. As they came into full view again, one roughly pulled and cut the thorn-bushes, and the second finely shaped their ends to keep the sheep in—and sheep thieves out. They both turned their heads to look at her: one doffed his cap, while the other bowed and smiled.

Next walked three farmers and a fisherman. One of the farmers pulled a cart full of raw barley. Two had axles over their shoulders with large baskets on either side. One had baskets full of onions and turnips, while the other had cabbages and pease. The fisherman had a large covered basket on his shoulder with the tail of fish just sticking out of the top beneath the lid. Sweating with labor, they didn't smile or pause, but nodded politely if formally as they caught Marie's eye. They passed a small stream where poor girls washed and thrashed laundry and hung it on lines draped between wooden poles.

As the road curved up and back to the right, a round-faced and round-bodied man dressed in loose pantaloons and a long, beige tunic sat on a barrel at the corner just off the road, offering ladles full of water from another large barrel to passersby. He held up the ladle to Marie, and she watched some water drip off and plash onto the dust of the road below. The man shook his head wryly and winked at Marie. Image that: he winked! Then he handed the ladle to the fisherman, who had just reached the point where he was sitting at the turn of the road. The fisherman up-turned the ladle and took a long drink, then brushed his chin with his sleeve. He heaved a long sigh—he actually sighed aloud—and nodded to waterman and handed him a small coin.

"*Non nobis nomine, Domine*": ahead on the second level brown-robed monks and black-cloaked nuns chanted together as they walked with their heads bowed. One of the monks, a tall, reedy older man with a wispy grey beard and a toothy smile stopped and looked kindly at Marie and made the sign of the Cross. Without thinking that she was doing so, Marie signed to, in reply, and the monk nodded vigorously and continued on his way. Ahead of them a wheelwright had stopped by the side of the road to mend a wheel for a carter. Three carpenters with their tools in open-topped wooden boxes strode up the hill for their work at the castle, a cooper and a carver were talking shop, and a man in high boots had stopped at a wooden shed to talk with another man who was sitting there mending fishing nets. Two men in long cloaks and tall hats talked closely about the current cost of wines from France and Italy and the difficulty of shipping them safely. A group of five young women, just at the far edge of girlhood, stopped in a small apple orchard to fill their baskets with fruit. They smiled and sang a folk song about a young man who had died for love of a beautiful girl.

Near the corner of the second level stood several outbuildings or barns: among them one housed a blacksmith, one a tanner, one a dyer. Their skin had darkened, stained with their trades, and their hands and forearms were well muscled, sleeves rolled up to their elbows for work. The smith's harmer fell with an insistent, resounding, rhythmic ring as he pounded thin metal straps to wrap around barrels to hold the wooden slats together. Marie saw a barn for work-horses, but there she saw also a young nobleman dressed in blue, probably a second son, who was talking with one of the ostlers about getting a fresh shoe for his stallion.

Just beyond the turn now stood a number of shops— a butcher, candlers, bakers, brewers, two sewing shops and a haberdasher, a hatter, and a shoemaker—the whole of the array seemed to have shifted forward along the road and up the hill, as if the whole world were changing shape and order. The shops had buyers and sellers arguing, haggling prices, or just stopping in their work to tell jokes and stories. As Marie tried to make out what some of them were saying, they all turned around at once and smiled and waved to her! She found herself waving back unconsciously.

Then something ahead caught her attention, and she saw where men and women were sitting together in a lovely field of flowers and mown grass listening to a minstrel who had just tuned his rebec and begun to sing a love song: clean-shaven, he wore a wide, floppy hat with a tall feather sticking up from it, and beside him sat three village girls who sang or hummed along softly with counterpoints to his tune. When they had finished, the nobles, intent on his song, for the voices were youthful and fine, all called out their appreciation, and some few tossed small coins into sack the minstrel had left open at his feet. The noble ladies called for another song, so he began, though this time he looked directly at Marie as though he was singing for her.

> Western wind, when wilt thou blow,
> that the small rain down can rain?
> Christ, that my love were in my arms
> and I in my bed again. . . .

Marie blushed at the words, and a muted "Oh!" just escaped her lips, and she hurried her glance ahead to where the gates opened to the town, where tournament and banquet fields stretched up toward the castle keep. There knights were checking their gear and helping one another to tighten their armor, and squires were helping them prepare their horses and weapons. But something looked different about them: to her eye they did not look so much like soldiers as like sportsmen, not men trained to kill in pitched combat, but men eager to win in sport and game. And at the far end of the field ladies had gathered to test their skills in archery! She noticed again at the very top of castle the lord and lady looking out the window. They had changed their clothing: the lady wore lace and frills around the cuffs and neck of her red gown decorated with bright stones, and she wore her hair fanned out broadly, with a wide black hat with a white silk flourish atop it. The lord wore a thick black and white jacket, his pointed beard falling down to his chest, and he had black otter-skin gloves and a wide-brimmed white hat with a very large black feather to top it off. The two of them looked at Marie, seemed to have been looking at her for some time, and they both nodded as if to confirm her thought: sportsmen, and sportswomen, who have not seen battle—they compete for the pleasure of it and to remember the old times.

Marie believed she had heard them say those words: "to remember the old times."

Then she heard that sound again: that high-pitched mechanical, metallic wail. Hoo—oot, hoot, hoot, hoo—oot, hoot! And she turned her glance from the castle back to the bottom left of the tapestry.

There stood the young man again, looking at her and smiling, but he looked very different this time. His dress had changed: Marie had never seen or imagined such clothing. He wore sturdy black leather boots and black trousers that went all the way down to his feet. Over a white shirt he had a grey wool vest that fit tightly to his torso and came just below his waist. Draped from one pocket of the vest to another lay a silver chain. Around his neck he had a band of dark red cloth that tucked into his vest, and he had a black jacket, open in front, that fell just down to his hips. In one hand he held a tall, black cylindrical device with a short brim, which he then placed on his head, giving it a quick tap downward with his hand—a strange sort of hat indeed, and hardly practical looking for the height it stood above his head.

He smiled broadly at Marie and tugged one end of the silver chain across his middle, drawing a round, silver, metallic object from one of the pockets. He looked intently at one side of it, then looked up with an expression of surprise.

"Time!" he said, and he motioned for Marie to follow him.

The scene ahead had changed. A long, grey walkway led to short building of what looked like smooth stone. Then she heard that strange howl again: a ghostly hooting that slid from one pitch to another, but this time a loud chugging sound followed, and then a high-pitched metallic whine, and a sound of heavy metal grinding and dropping to halt, and then a loud puff. Waves of white smoke billowed to Marie's left and briefly covered the young man who walked through and motioned to her again to join him near the strangest contraption she had ever seen:

a huge, heavy cylindrical compartment leading back to a high window with a man looking out. He had one hand placed on a lever inside the contraption, and with the other hand he waved familiarly to Marie. He tugged down on the lever, and the whistle sung out again, accompanied by another great puff of white smoke that blew away above the compartment.

Unconsciously she draw her hand up to her throat—how familiarly these men treated her! But she couldn't keep her eyes from following along to the right as the rest of what must have been an enormous infernal war machine tumbled up behind. After the first came several more compartments, rectangular in shape and made apparently of wood and metal, connected serially. These closed compartments had many windows, and inside she could see the silhouettes of men and women seated in rows. The men had mostly round, domish hats and dark suits like the young man at the beginning of the tapestry, and the women had dresses of black or grey or off-white decorated with draped or gathered cloth or lace of various sorts and accented with pins and other jewelry of stones of many bright colors. They did not look up, but seemed to sit in conversations among themselves, though some held before them large sheets something lighter than vellum with pictures and writing, and they perused those objects with critical frowns.

The young man had leaped onto the steps of the second of those carts. With one hand he grasped a bar that allowed him to hang partly out of the cart; with the other he had removed his tall hat and was using it to wave Marie to follow him into the carriage!

From the huge, impossible object came a loud snort, a deep metallic grunt a hiss of steam that nearly enshrouded it in white smoke.

Marie looked above to the upper layers of the tapestry. They stood clothed in a cloud from the great war engine, but from what she could see through the smoke, they too had transformed. She saw rows of buildings, fields, long structures with the sounds of activity coming from them, and lines of people dressed in trousers and half-length coats entering them. The lawns had turned into packed masses of cubicle shapes, residences and shops of all sort, most dismal, but some bright and appealing, all encircled in a mist of dun-colored, oily smelling air.

She hesitated just an instant, and once again the young man pulled out the silver circle from his pocket and glanced at it. "Time!" he called to Marie. "Hurry if you want to see!"

Forgetting that she had been standing before a tapestry hung from the sturdiest of walls, she stepped as the young man bade her up toward that noisy, frightening carriage.

What an adventure!

He held out his hand, and she reached up and felt the firmness of his flesh. He grasped her palm confidently and drew her up into the carriage.

"All aboard!" he called out loudly behind them as they entered the carriage.

With several more hoots and cloud upon cloud of white smoke, the carriage jolted ahead: Marie grasped an upright bar to steady herself, and the young man held on to her hand to help her brace against the movement.

The magical carriage propelled itself ahead at the pace of a trotting horse, but was gradually increasing its pace. Marie felt dizzy with its movement and the dim world of the carriage, lit only by dull daylight and a smoky haze from several lamps that seemed to burn something slick and oily. She had to stifle a cough.

"Welcome! Come and sit here by these people. Listen! They won't mind. They're glad you've come!" The young man led Marie to a short bench behind several of the other passengers and guided her in to sit down. A few of the others nodded curt greetings, but even they returned to their conversations or the viewing of the manuscripts they had unfolded before them. One man read through two round, glass opticals held to his head by a thin metal band that wrapped around his ears. He read as though he would bore a hole in his manuscript. "Enjoy your travels, Ma'am," the young man said, bowing slightly from the waist. He placed his hat on a rack that ran along the carriage above the passengers, and he passed along the length of the carriage and exited through its back door.

Before Marie could allow a rising glint of fear to overtake her, she found herself caught up in the conversation of two women seated directly in front of her. They sat facing her and spoke in low tones so that no other passengers could hear, but she could follow the words, which they made no effort to conceal from her.

How can I understand them? she wondered. They are not speaking my language. It sounds like the English tongue, but different: sharper, quicker, higher vowels, and hesitating consonants. They wore long, beige dresses with puffed shoulders and with vests pulled tight at the waist and clinging to the bosom, and brown leather gloves and almost conical hats wrapped around with thin, gauzy cloth to hold them on. They had dark brown shoes that tapered to a point at the toes and tall, thin spikes for heels. Before she could complete her thoughts, she was unequivocally listening.

"Mina, what is troubling you? I thought you'd be happy, going to Lucy's wedding," said the first lady, touching the wrist of her companion.

"It's my sister Belle, you know, Effie. I always knew she was headed for trouble in love. She was such a beau'ful baby, and she's only got more beautiful as she's grown up. She don't put on airs, but she has that way of walking with her chin up and firm, as ladylike as anyone. She met

Lord"—and here the woman whispered low—"Hampstead when he brought his Intended to the hat shop."

"Oh, Mina, they say he's such a handsome man, Lord Hampstead"—Effie also whispered. "Did you get to see him?"

"You're right, I did," Mina responded, "and he surely is. Slim and shapely, tall but not too tall, with a sparkle of the devil in those angelic eyes. You can bet I looked up from my work that day."

The carriage hit a rough spot, rattling and jostling the passengers. Its shook Marie dreadfully, but none of the others seemed the least bit troubled. Away from where she had begun her journey, she looked out the window, and the air had cleared. The carriage, chugging rapidly, seemed to fly past scenes of activity: boys running about and tossing and kicking a ball around a field; a stream with long, low boats pulled along with ropes by equine beasts; sheepfields with long, curving stone fences; farms bejeweling the gently rolling emerald slopes. Then the voices again took hold of her thoughts.

"I don't think at first he meant anything by it, but he treated Belle kindly and even kissed her hand when she handed over the hat—and it was one fine piece of work, I can tell you. He looked like he did it without thinking, Effie, and then he even blushed—I think he hoped his Intended hadn't seen him do it, and she hadn't, as she was talking with Miss Pedigrew about some gloves and kerchiefs that she had about the shop to match."

"They always start that way, young lords do, Mina, at least the nicer ones. Behavin' gently, no evil intentions, but that's not how things always turn out. And not all of them are so nice."

"Don't I know it, dear. And what a surprise when he came back a week later, alone: he said he wanted to buy more gloves and kerchiefs and some knick-knacks that Miss Pedigrew keeps about—she's a smart one and knows how to do business with customers.

"Well, he asked particularly for Belle, said he admired her taste and wanted her for consultation, and so Belle helped him pick out all sorts of things for the Intended, to go with other outfits, and he assured Belle he couldn't thank her enough for her splendid advice, and might he not just do something for her by way of thanks, but she demurred, saying she was glad to help with gifts for so fine a lady, and she wished they might find every happiness together, and he finally and very reluctantly left the shop, turning for one more glance at Belle as the door closed behind him.

"You can be sure that by then Miss Pedigrew thought Lord Hampstead the finest of gentlemen and dear Belle the finest shopgirl ever. On the lord's orders she sent arms-full of packages not to the Intended's home, but to the family villa in Dover, where she would be returning after a month's stay in France to enjoy the Fall weather there. He had taken particular care to mention that month, and to mention it within Belle's hearing.

"I daresay that's not the last time you saw him in the shop," added Effie knowingly.

"Right again, Effie dear."

"But things turned out all right, didn't they, Mina? And what of poor Charley, who was reading law at the Inns of Court? He was always after her, wanting to be her steady beau, weren't he?"

"That's as you'll have to judge for yourself. I think I've told you before that Belle is awfully good with gadgets?'

"Gadgets?" Effie asked.

"Inventions, you know: she makes things, things no one's ever seen or thought of before. She's been doing it since she was just a lass, out in her father's tool shed—he's a good craftsman himself, and Belle seems to have inherited it. Well here's what happened—I think I have just enough time to tell you the whole thing before the train reaches London."

Train, Marie thought. Yes, one might call it that. She thought of the engine in the front and the companion seating cars streaming along behind.

Marie had turned her face to the window, not wanting to intrude on her fellow passengers' conversation but desperate to hear what had happened with Belle. She watched the landscape change from rural to small town to the unimaginable filth and grandeur of London as the story unfolded.

Just as Belle had always been a beautiful girl, so had Charles Wright always loved her. They both came from the rising Middle Class, the energy and bolster that held together the stark and now unsteady social gulf between England's landed, hereditary elite and its shiftless grossly poor. Belle had confidence, but not born alone of beauty: she had an easy kindness with people, wit to stay clear of dangers, and a willingness to work in a trade that would neither enrich nor demean her. Charles' family came from the old guild class, but his father had wanted his hard-working son to move beyond the limitations of his caste and upbringing. He had by means of good business relations with influential clients of his carriage making and repair business argued eager young Charles into a law readership in the Temple district of London. Charles was a good-hearted lad with the wit to succeed, but he had always suffered from a defect in confidence. He had gravitated to Belle from early childhood, but had never managed to express his feelings for her beyond tokens of his admiration and friendship. He hoped—and his father hoped, knowing the lad's heart—that a proper legal career might put him in a professional place and stoke his courage sufficiently that he might finally approach Belle with a declaration of love.

Nearing the end of his studies, and with a position promised him—not in London, but in Canterbury, not so bad a place to start—Charles had nearly arrived at the courage to tell Belle how he felt about her.

Now Belle did not lack sensitivity, and she knew, had known, Charles' feelings since they were children. She had never spoken of it herself, partly because she didn't want to shock the poor boy, but also partly because she didn't feel certain of her own feelings: she had always *liked* Charles, but didn't know if she could say that she *loved* him. She knew him as an honorable but sometimes precipitous young man and feared he might propose marriage without the two of them carefully considering the preliminaries. She wanted first to talk with him as, she thought, Lord Hampstead must have talked with his Intended—she was sure a man like that must know how to court a girl officially and at a proper pace, with families and friends approving. Such a man would neither submit to a match that family had arranged, nor would he assume the girl would accept his proposal without working up to it in stages.

Lord Hampstead was quite a catch for Miss Pedigrew as a client. Among the most dashing bachelors-soon-to-be-wed among London's socialites, he had a reputation for good looks, for generosity bordering on excess, and as a sportsman: he had won awards at Oxford for crew, archery, and shooting, having been the top pistol shot in his class.

Sadly, Charles, dressed in his best suit, appeared at Miss Pedigrew's haberdashery just as Lord Hampstead had come to call on Belle to take her to lunch. *She* assumed that Lord Hampstead must have come *just* to consult her further about additional presents for the Intended, while *he* assumed that by now she must have more than an inkling of his growing affections. The two them stepped out into the street, Belle looking very tall with her hair dressed high on her head and a grey-blue hat sitting atop like a crown, and Hampstead looked dashing, rich, and very self-assured. Charles assumed that Belle had allowed her affections to fall upon Hampstead, and the thought troubled him deeply. He nearly determined to follow them, then nearly decided out of despair to return to work, and then finally turned on his heels, pulled his wide-brimmed American-style hat down over his eyes, and indeed followed them about half a block behind.

"Where shall we go?" Belle asked.

"The Georgian," Hampstead replied, "best restaurant in this part of town."

Lord Hampstead had tried to circle Belle's arm around his, but she deftly brushed his arm away and plunged ahead walking at a great pace so that he had to make an effort to keep up. She felt glad that she had remained cautious. The Georgian was well known for its food, but also as a place for lovers' trysts. Belle had tipped Robin, the dustman at Miss Pedigrew's, to follow her to wherever Lord Hampstead should take her and to bring with him a device she had made in the tool shed. While she found the man charming, and he might well have in mind no more than he had said, she distrusted his impulses just enough to take precautions.

She had taken the smallest Daguerreotype camera she could find, a cast-off from a local photographer, and attached beneath it an expandable device made of strips of metal bolted at angles to a hand-sized crank. One could raise or lower the camera by about three and a half feet, and so hide behind a barrier, raise the camera above it, and take a picture of someone beyond the partition without being seen—as long as one could disguise the flash and sound the camera made with the photograph. Belle smiled, thinking that while The Georgian must seem a safe place to Hampstead and other men of his class, it was also famous as a place for couples to have their pictures taken by photographers to have as keepsakes. She would have a camera there, but not for any purpose Lord Hampstead might have in mind.

At the Georgian Lord Hampstead had reserved with the Maître'd to seat them at a table away from the front windows and toward the back of the dining room in an area partitioned with plants and decorated Shoji screens. Fortunately for Belle, one of the screens was both opaque and sturdy enough to be perfect for Robin: Belle had given him money to tip the waiter, and Robin told him that the couple had asked him to take a photograph to celebrate their engagement, but to do so without disturbing the other diners. Robin stood hidden and quietly cranked up the camera so that it sat just above with a view downward toward the table.

Lord Hampstead ordered for the two of them: caviar and champagne, oysters and chardonnay, and a cutlet on greens accompanied by a *Corton Renardes* from the Côtes de Beaune.

Charles, following unobtrusively and arriving at The Georgian just after Belle and Hampstead, tipped the Maître d' and asked if he might not go into the dining room to look for his mother, who he was sure was dining there and might have forgotten her physician's appointment. He positioned himself between two large ferns and watched as Lord Hampstead plied Belle with rich wines and tried repeatedly to take her hand. Belle repeatedly withdrew her hand and sat straight-baked, blushing, eating enough to be polite and only sipping at her wine glass—she had had very little experience with alcohol. Charles felt sure that he heard Hampstead whispering his love and devotion to Belle, and he felt equally sure that he had heard Belle repeatedly reminding him of his lovely and faithful Intended.

Before he could draw attention to himself, Charles decided on his course of action and left, thanking the Maître d' on his way out, protesting that his mother must have remembered her appointment and so not have appeared as scheduled for lunch.

Just then, with a brief thump and puff of smoke Robin got a picture of Belle with her hands raised before her deflecting Hampstead's expression of affection. Robin quickly withdrew the camera and, with the waiter's help, exited out the back door of The Georgian into an alley and hurried back to the haberdashery.

"What was that?" Hampstead asked

"A photograph," Belle said, "over there. See the couple sitting there—you can just see them though the break in the screens. They have had a photograph done, probably to celebrate a birthday or anniversary. I hear that happens quite commonly at The Georgian."

He believed her. To speak fairly of Lord Hampstead, who was seldom so gullible, he did indeed seem smitten with Belle, and he vigorously professed that he had fallen in love with her, would communicate the same to the previous intended immediately upon her return to England, and would remain loving and faithful to Belle all his days. He may well have meant all he said, but Belle could hardly trust such a rapid change in his affections. She assured him that, while she admired him and felt honored that he should bestow such manly feelings upon her, she did also hold his Intended in great respect and affections, and that her own affections had but lately settled on another young man. She had accompanied him to lunch only to help Hampstead with the selection of such items as might best please that lovely lady. Lord Hampstead finally sat back in his chair, rubbed his chin, and sighed. He betrayed anger only once: when Belle spooned out the last of the caviar and delicately licked her lips with its savor—the caviar had been very expensive indeed.

After lunch Belle insisted on taking a Hackney cab back to Miss Pedigrew's, for which Lord Hampstead gallantly paid after one more failed attempt to take her hand. She assured him that Miss Pedigrew deeply valued his condescension to do business at her shop and would be glad to help him again any time, and he assured her that he held nothing against Miss Pedigrew or her and would certainly return despite his broken heart.

"Think on your Intended," Belle assured him, "whom I'm certain you truly love, and all will be well with you again. I wish you both the best of happiness!" She did permit him to shake her hand formally, and he said good-bye, she felt from beneath his sleeve an uncharacteristic touch distinctly identifiable as lace. Off she rode with the intention of completing her afternoon's designs and then developing Robin's film in the back room at Miss Pedigrew's.

Meanwhile, Charles had walked hard to the closest train station and had taken and Underground past St. Paul's over to the east end of Whitechapel. In the dark, mildewed, fog-hidden alleys below street level the informed person undaunted by personal danger could find any number odd shops stocked with curiosities and specialty items. One could find humans, too, or something like them, of all shapes and desires and in all sorts of phantasmagorical dress and speaking any sort of language. At a military pawn shop he purchased a used Webley-Pryse revolver along with only with two rounds and slipped them into his jacket pockets. The proprietor made no inquiries about his training or purposes, because Charles paid full price in cash.

Not by nature or practice a violent man, Charles had grown up around men who had military experience and did not mind talking about it. His grandfather had campaigned in China in the First Opium War in 1839, and his father had fought in Crimea in the mid '50s. Charles himself had spent six months in the Transvaal as a medic during the Boer War; there he had learned to shoot but also the consequences of shooting and had resoled to return home to read law instead or studying medicine. He felt that he had one last use for his knowledge of firearms.

The next day just before noon Lord Hampstead appeared again at Miss Pedigrew's. He was carrying a basket of flowers and fruit which he asked one of the clerks to deliver to Belle, and he bought a few scented handkerchiefs and a hatpin in addition to all the items on a list that Belle had prepared for him the day before

Miss Pedigrew beamed.

Belle came out from the workshop in back and shook Lord Hampstead's hand and assured him that his Intended would feel very pleased with the gifts and that she hoped the two of them would find extraordinary happiness together.

Lord Hampstead looked a little deflated, but he remained gracious, thanking Belle and Miss Pedigrew and all the clerks in the showroom.

Belle felt sure that she would not see him again accept perhaps as a customer or just in passing, but London was a very large city with very many people, and human events do take odd courses. She had in her bag in the back room a photograph of herself rejecting Lord Hampstead's affections and also a finely sharpened and especially sturdy letter opener, which she now felt sure she wouldn't need, but planned to keep them just in case.

Belle watched through the front window as Lord Hampstead left and turned to wave one final good-bye when she saw a man wearing a formal black suit and a wide-brimmed American-style hat come up to him. Of all persons, it was Charles! She couldn't hear their conversation, but it went like this.

"I beg your pardon: Lord Hampstead?"

"Yes. Have we met? I don't believe I recognize you." The nobleman puffed his just chest out just a bit and met Charles eye to eye.

"No, sir, I don't think there's any reason why you would know me. I greet you cordially but seriously and will take only a moment of your time. My name is Charles

Wright, and I read law at the Temple. I know that you have a loving fiancée, though I met her only once when I wrote some papers legal papers for her father as an apprentice to my master. I would not do her such a discourtesy as to speak of her except to say that I regard her as an admirable women. I speak also as a friend of Belle Holmwood: respectfully I tell you that I saw you yesterday professing love to her, and I would not have her or your Intended hurt in any way for the whole world in exchange. Here is my card: I request your presence tomorrow morning, at your convenience, for a duel after the old fashion, and I hope you will accommodate me. I have not had the benefit of any training with the sword, but will otherwise accept the weapon of your choice. I must tell you that as a former military man I have some skill with a revolver, but not unusual ability for a man of my station and experience."

It was quite a long speech for Charles to make and for Lord Hampstead to listen to.

Imagine a commoner speaking so to a knight!

"Are you mad, young man?"

"No, sir, I don't believe so. But I am in deadly earnest."

"Do you know that I am a fine shot with a pistol or a rifle?"

"Yes, sir, I have heard that."

"And you would quarrel with me anyway?"

"Quarrel, sir? No. I intend simply to defend the honor of two exceedingly fine ladies—or I should say women. Miss Hampstead may not be noble by birth, but she is every bit a lady to me, if you'll forgive my saying so."

"I say," Lord Hampstead said, rubbing his chin. "Well, if I must, then I must. You have a pistol, do you?"

"Yes, sir."

"And you want to meet tomorrow morning. Where? You know that dueling has been illegal for two hundred years? You know also that you are not of my class, and so I have no obligation to you and could readily have you arrested."

"Yes, sir, I know. I am relying on your honor. Please feel welcome to choose the place. I have no intention to inconvenience you."

"But you do intend to shoot me? Ah, I'm beginning to understand now. You must be the young man Miss Holmwood spoke fondly of. You and she have an understanding?"

"No, sir. If you will forgive my bluntness, I have had a great affection for her since we were children, but have always considered her above me."

"You are reading law now."

"Yes, sir. My father is a carriage maker, but he wanted me to try to better myself."

"Nothing wrong with carriage-making as a profession."

"Nothing at all, sir: I quite agree. He wished me to take up an intellectual profession. I served as a medic in the

Boer War, and after stitching up wounds decided that law would be better."

"Yes, I see what you mean. And will you stitch me up after you shoot me?"

"I doubt that shall be necessary."

"And who will stitch you up if I shoot you?"

"That, too, must go as it shall."

"*Que sera, sera?*"

"Exactly, sir."

"Then I agree to meet you tomorrow morning at seven at the north end of the park beyond Highgate. Does that suit you? Let's make it pistols, since you seem comfortable with that."

"Very good. Thank you, sir." Charles dipped his head in a bow and walked on back to the train station to return to the Temple.

"Extraordinary, and on the Heath of all places," Lord Hampstead said aloud. So this is man upon whom Belle has bestowed her affection, he thought, and he turned to walk to his club.

When Lord Hampstead had appeared, Robin had got an odd itch in his left ear that had left him feeling something was about to go wrong. He slipped out the back door of the haberdashery and was standing just around the corner of the building listening to the conversation between the two men. Fortunately for him Charles had not raised his head when he had walked by, and Lord Hampstead had gone the other way.

Robin went right to Belle and told her everything he had heard.

When Belle left work, she went right to Charles' family's home to look for him. They hadn't seen him, so she went to his rooms near St. Paul's accompanied by her younger brother and his friends. He wasn't there, either. Belle went home to wait for news while she sent the boys all over the city looking for Charles, but they couldn't find him.

Charles spent the whole night walking. Thinking that might be his last night on earth, he had gone to get his Webley-Pryse and then had thrown himself out into the cool, misty London night. He watched people walking, saw them through windows as they dined, watched them board coaches coming from the theatres. He thought of the private, self-propelled coach, the "auto-mobile" his father claimed he would one day design, a carriage not requiring a horse and much smaller than a train, borne about with its own engine. Then he dived into the train tunnels and absorbed their smoke-and-oil perfume, let the sounds of the train cars rattle his bones to help him shake off the cold. Finally he caught the last train to the north of town and got out and walked through Highgate to—he had forgotten the name, how ironic!—Hampstead Heath. He thought he observed a youth on a bicycle who appeared to be following him at a distance. A fine cycle it was, too: lean and quick to maneuver, with low handlebars to keep the rider in a racing position, unlike any he had seen—but he thought passed from his mind as he considered the duel no more than an hour ahead.

Charles crossed the Heath and reached the north end—not a mile from Keats' home, he thought—and got there as he heard the toll of a half-hour bell: six-thirty, he thought. He should be on time.

By six-forty-five he had placed himself in a spot noticeable to someone who was looking for him but otherwise unobtrusive, under some trees. The few casual passers-by didn't notice him as they scurried or lumbered off to work. In a few minutes he heard a voice.

"You chose the spot I was thinking of," said the voice, and Lord Hampstead appeared out of the morning gloom.

"Thank you for coming, sir," Charles said.

"I have no wish to disappoint you, young man, or myself. You have brought no second?" Lord Hampstead asked.

"No, I beg your pardon—I didn't think of it."

"I will be his second," said a youthful voice, as the boy whom Charles had seen following him on the bicycle appeared from behind a tree. "If you will permit me." A slim lad, he was dressed in a long dark coat and a floppy hat.

"Of course. Thank you!"

"I have brought only a trusted servant," Hampstead said. "May I see your weapon?"

Charles handed him the revolver.

"Very nice," Hamsptead said. "A Webley-Pryse, no? Here is mine, a Lancaster Pistol." He handed it to Charles. "All right with you?"

"Yes, certainly. I have never done this before, but . .
.

"And you must not do it now! Are you mad? Apologize and go home before it is too late!" the youth had grabbed both his arms from behind and hissed in his ear.

"You're very kind, but I have asked for this appointment myself and so must and will go through with it."

"Why, why are you doing this?" the youth was nearly crying.

"For the honor of two ladies."

"Two? Who is the other one?"

"The other one? Which is the *other* one?" Charles asked, beginning to recognize the voice.

"Come on, then," Lord Hampstead said. "How do you prefer to proceed: back to back and pace off?"

"I hadn't thought of that. I assumed we would do what the Americans do: draw and shoot."

"Americans? Do you have a hip-holster for your revolver?"

"No. Won't a pocket do?"

"Probably not easy to draw from that. What say we hold the pistols down facing the ground, and one of our seconds will count, and on the speaking of the number three, we shall raise our weapons and shoot."

"I won't do it!" screamed the youth. The voice now sounded like that of a woman, and a familiar woman at that.

Hampstead's servant stepped forward. "I will do the count."

"That all right with you?" Hampstead asked Charles. "I don't want you to feel as though I have an advantage. Thank you, Theo."

"Quite fair of you, sir," Charles said. "Shall we begin?"

"No!" called the woman's voice.

"Before we draw more attention," Hampstead said. A few passersby had begun to filter toward them from the streets, hearing voices at such an odd time of the morning. "Not quite seven yet."

"On your man's count, sir," Charles said.

Charles steadied his feet: the ground was still wet from the past evening's rain, though the sky had cleared with the first morning light.

When Theo spoke three, Charles' second screamed, and both men without raising their arms fired their pistols into the wet ground at their feet.

"You had no intention of shooting me, Mr. Wright?" Hampstead asked.

"No, sir, I never did. For me it was only a point of honor, though I'm a commoner. I don't think we should treat the women we love as playthings—forgive me for bluntness. I called you out only to show you how much that point matters to me."

"Not so common, I think, and you have taught me a good lesson about men as well as women. I thank you for it. I hope you feel that honor is satisfied? Good man. But look to it: I think your second has fainted."

Charles turned, and the "lad" had indeed fallen to the ground in a faint, his cap beside him. Charles bent over and lifted the head, wet from the turf, from the ground. The morning light was clear enough the he recognized the face of his beloved Belle.

He stroked her cheek lightly.

Hampstead came over and offered Charles his hip flask. "See if you can get a sip of brandy in her. It can sometimes revive—but I'm sure you learned that in the war. Is that who I think it is?" he asked, looking more closely.

"Yes. Thank you." Charles took the brandy, wet his fingers with it, and touched them to Belle's lips. Her eyes opened, and at first they showed joy—the joy turned, as she revived, to anger.

"Charles, you are indeed the stupidest of men! You could have been killed. What did you hope to accomplish here?"

"What I did accomplish, I think," he said, turning to Lord Hampstead.

"Indeed you have, young man. I hope only that you haven't by teaching me lost the love of someone far more important to you. Did you really believe, Miss Holmwood, that I would shoot him?"

On that day and for many days Belle could express only anger at Charles, but eventually she came around, realizing his devotion, and at their wedding they received a lovely gift from Lord Hampstead: a silver brandy flask and two small, gold drinking bowls. Soon after their wedding,

Belle and Charles heard of Lord Hampstead's marriage to his Intended; they sent sp   ecially designed hats from Miss Pedigrew's shop for the noble couple.

Shortly after they were married, Belle invested her savings from working at Miss Pedigrew's in Charles' fathers' plans for a self-propelling carriage.

It did not pay off so well for them, but it paid off very well for their children, who managed thereby to become wealthy from the production and sale of automobiles.

* * *

Marie looked up to see that the train had stopped and that once again large billowing clouds of smoke had enveloped it. The wild hoot was calling out its now familiar refrain.

"All aboard, London to Dover!" called the young man. "Mind the stairs." Entering the carriage, he came straight for Marie. He carried a sack that he handed her. "From a favorite bakery," he said. "Scones—my mother's favorites—and in the cup you'll find a splendid black tea, which I hope is still at least warm. We'll make Dover in no time today: fine, clear weather and few stops. Please relax and enjoy the ride." He smiled and tipped his tall hat.

Marie felt the remarkable warmth of the tea, and she bit into one of the scones: buttery and smooth, honey-sweet and chewy, perfectly matched with the warming tea, with tiny hints of lightness and bitter.

"Vanilla and orange icing," the young man said, and dried currants inside. Yes, my mother's favorites!"

The train made a small jolt and began its trek to Dover with a hoot and a chug as Marie savored her scone. She thought of these lines, which came to her from the metallic turning of the train's enormous wheels:

Adventures come in tales or dreams,
 Likewise true or mad, it seems.
The Bretons turned them both to lais,
 Some for pay, some just to please.
They share them by a Christmas fire
Or hide them like a deep desire.
How much will the lady tell,
How much assume some evil spell?

From the rear of the carriage Marie heard a woman gently singing "'Tis So Sweet to Trust in Jesus." The song pleased her and began to make her feel sleepy.

One must know amethyst from porphyry, she thought, not knowing what she meant by it.

* * *

"Sister. Sister!"

Marie heard the voice beside her and felt a hand on her elbow. Startled, she looked to see Henry there beside her with a smile of uncertainly on his face and a tall, lit taper in his hand.

"Henry! What are you doing here!"

"I? I live here. And you are my guest. And it's an hour before dawn, and you were standing here asleep on your feet before my tapestries. Look, your tapir's gone out. What in the world are *you* doing here?"

"Asleep?" Marie said. "Was I in asleep? Henry, I have had the most extraordinary experience."

"Of what?"

"Of this tapestry. I was examining it in the firelight, and suddenly it . . . it . . .

"It what?" Henry asked.

Then Marie, waking more fully to her senses, wondered what she was going to tell Henry—or even *how* to tell him what she had seen. And she wondered what she had seen: much of it made no sense to her.

"I don't think I was sleeping. I saw something. Henry, I must tell you—but no one else—about it."

"What did you see?"

"Hmmm. It is not so easy to describe. But it was extraordinary."

"I have heard of such things with poets," Henry said. "Dreaming of stories. Have you a new Romance to tell, given you by the angel of dreams?"

"Yes! No. Maybe—I'm not sure. I must think it through to determine how to tell it, if I can understand it. Oh, Henry, what a frightening, amazing tapestry!"

"This one? It has inspired you, eh? Well, then, it turns out to be worth the great cost and trouble I spent to get it. Quite the temperamental craftsman, and then once he finished it, he didn't want to give it up. I had to lean on him, and I paid him extra. Don't know what he'd have done with it if I hadn't paid and had let him keep it—not a wealthy man, you know. But look at you: your skin's white with cold—how long have you been standing here? You could at least have pulled up a chair to sit down. I have heard of soldiers sleeping on their feet in a pinch, but never of a storytelling nun doing so. You must get more diligent in your prayers perhaps, ha?"

"Yes, perhaps I must—a sad fault in a nun."

"If you ask me, you should never have become one, but I know I'm not supposed to talk about that anymore. What's done is done, and I'm glad you're here, and I want nothing more for you than that you are happy. But go along now: up to bed with you before you freeze. Look, the fire's nearly out. I'll box the ears of the fellow sleeping over there. Huh: he's heard me talking, and look how he jumps to his feet to tend it now. I am going for a hot drink, then out for a walk to wait for sun-up—the sky is clear, and it should be beautiful this morning. No, you're not coming along: I won't have you going back ill, or you won't come back for next Christmas with more stories, and I depend on that. Wouldn't be Christmas without one of Marie's lais for all the court to hear. Up you go before someone else see's you padding about the castle in the dark. We'll talk later, and you shall tell me a new story."

Henry gave a little shove on Marie's elbow to push her toward the stairway. He grunted a laugh and strode toward the pantry, pulling his cloak up around his neck.

"Chilly indeed this morning. Go on: back to bed!"

Marie shivered, noticed that her candle had in fact gone out—she wondered how long ago. Arnolf was guiltily re-stoking the fire, so that even from a distance it already gave a hint of heat and a burst of light so that she could see her way back up the staircase.

She glanced back at the tapestry. It looked shadowy and dull in the growing firelight, but the figures stood still as an empty fire-grate. There stood the young man in the lower left, unmoving, and there his companions, just as the weaver had shaped them. She heard no horses, no conversations, no *trains*. She thought she tasted a hint of orange and currants on her tongue.

I must find a story in my memory, Marie thought, one that they have not heard. No one will believe this one, the one I think I saw, if I even can make a lai of it. But what a Christmas story it would make!

Sleeping, dreaming—is that all it was?

She yawned, covered her mouth. She shivered again and pulled her cloak tight, and she climbed the steps to return to her room to sleep. As she climbed she thought she heard from the banquet room—or imagined she heard it—a puff of steam. Must have been the fire in the hearth.

Only a Joust

BRIGHT AND CLEAR, THOUGH A CHILL RIDES IN THE breeze, thought Sir Lionel: a beautiful late-autumn afternoon had made a place for itself in December, nearly two months beyond its season. Thank God for the sunshine—the winter would roll in its ice and snow any day now.

The moon was already rising in the east even as the sun lingered, low in the southern sky. Two hours would pass before it cast its purple and orange tapestry over the western horizon.

Low clouds were skating in from the north, but they had a long swathe of open sky to cover yet. A prolonged autumn had kept its hold on summer's last warmth, and winter had merely whispered as it crept in, as if December's days enjoyed the balmy breezes and tempered light. Strong rains had fallen through November and had filled the rivers to the brim. Abundant water kept the green fields, not yet sere with the season, glowing silver, and the leaves had fallen late.

Yet as the wind kicked up in a soft swirl, Lionel could smell in it a hint of snow.

"Think of it," Lionel said aloud to no one, "nearly twelve hundred years since the birth of Our Lord. No horse runs faster than time."

He had ridden gently for perhaps an hour, perhaps two east of the castle, breathing deeply, enjoying the freedom of crisp air and open land. He knew Christmas lay soon ahead, but he had not yet got himself entirely clear on the dates since his release from imprisonment.

Twice two months before, the Duke of Metz had ridden with a small band of knights into Lionel's uncle's lands, which stretched along the Mosel south of Trier through the Rheinland to the Saarland in the east and Luxembourg in the west to the Disputed Lands in the south. The Duke made no secret of the fact that he coveted the territory all the way north to Trier. But he had no claim to those lands. He had ridden not with a harrying army, but with a small band of soldiers, good horseman and swordsmen, intent on reconnaissance, not battle. He wanted to know how much care Count Guillaume took of his lands, and like many of the region's noblemen, he resented the appointment of a Norman to oversee them, though they lay well beyond his own holdings.

But unexpectedly meeting

Sir Lionel with a small band of Guillaume's young knights training in a flat valley near the Disputed Lands, the Duke, rather than explain his presence so far north of his own holdings, had ridden directly on the young men, thinking to drive them off north. He cared no more for retreat than to explain his presence.

Though most of the South-Rhenish knights had little battle experience, they did not turn and run, but drew their weapons to meet the charge of the knights of Lorraine. They did so joyously, thinking to prove their courage and skill to their new overlord.

All of them fell with the exception of Lionel, by far the most experienced of them. With a head injury and a sword wound in his left side, he had kept his horse, unconscious in the saddle but alive. The victors wrapped his wounds, propped him upright on his horse, and took him back with them to Metz. The others they buried with Christian prayers and the honors due their chivalry.

Lionel should not even have been there among Franks, Allemans, and a few French lords: he had no quarrel with the Metzians. Born in Normandy, where even as a youth he fought raiders along the seacoast, he had accompanied his father to England when Henry II called him there. Henry himself had posted Lionel to the Roman Wall far in the north of Norman England. There he defended the King's lands against raiding parties and thieves and kept craftsmen and farmers from sneaking across to the north to sell their wares illegally—a relatively quiet post, but one where he had come to love the rolling green landscape with its stony hogback hills.

Hearing of his brother's border conflicts in Germania, Lionel's father had begged the King to send his son there with other young knights to reinforce his brother's position, dangerous lands he had been granted to hold as a reward for service to Henry VI Hohenstaufen. Lionel had gone neither entirely willingly nor unwillingly, but because his father so commanded: he owed and understood his duty both to his father and to his uncle.

When Lionel woke on the day after that battle four months past, he found himself captive in the Duke's castle in Metz.

He had a large, airy cell high up in the castle keep— no dungeon—with food and wine and clean water and even illuminated manuscripts to read and study. He had a servant who tended his wounds, trimmed his brown beard short after the Norman fashion, and forwarded his requests to the Duke, and for the first time in his life, Lionel felt glad that he knew how to read.

The jailor explained that Lionel's companions were all dead, and that the Duke grieved for it: he had intended no military expedition and hardly expected the obviously inexperienced knights would fight to the death. He had observed that Lionel, muscular and athletic though not a tall young man, had fought with astonishing vigor and courage, so he intended to treat him honorably and was currently negotiating for his release. One day the Duke himself had come: he praised Lionel for his resilience and assured him that before long he should get his freedom.

Two months later, Lionel's uncle Count Guillaume ransomed him, and the Duke of Metz had him escorted safely back to the border of southwestern Saarland. The captivity, while comparatively brief, had lasted longer than had Lionel hoped. Riding remained difficult and painful, but family concerns drove him to ride speedily as soon as his escort freed him.

Lionel returned to his uncle's castle to find that his wife of just under a year had died in childbirth the day before his arrival. He had got there in time to watch as she and their son were laid to rest in the castle crypt. Count Guillaume had ordered his stonemason to carve a bust of the young woman; Lionel noticed that he had captured even the small dimple in the center of his wife's chin and the way she swept her blonde hair over one shoulder.

Lionel fought a sense of emptiness by recalling that a year and a half ago he had not even met the girl, and a knight's duty to his lord outweighs any personal loss.

Yet he had loved her dearly, and each thought of her cut like a sword would to his heart.

Through two more months of convalescence, he had ridden daily in whatever direction had drawn him at the time. At first he had not ridden far and had not armed at all. But by the time of this particular December day, he was arming fully. He expected to meet no further skirmishes, but he felt the need to prepare as if he would. The Duke of Metz had paid weregild for the loss of the young men and had promised no further expeditions beyond the southern border of the Disputed Lands. But a good knight must remain prepared and keep in training. Lionel carried two spears and wore a sword at his side. He allowed himself no companions, preferring in his time of grief to ride alone.

Lionel felt a need for purpose, for activity, for a sense that his chivalry meant more than the continual distance from home and loss of friends and family, more than a daily ride among his uncle's beautiful but foreign fields and hills. That day his horse turned south and west of their usual course, as he had gave it freedom from the reins.

Topping a rise, he saw beyond a valley with a stream and a wood that stretched for what looked like many miles north, south, and east. The deciduous trees had dropped their leaves, which remained strewn in a broad, brown blanket, but these lands had enough evergreens that the wood still looked alive and active. The remnant greenness gave him a feeling of health, and it drew him.

He rode down to where the land turned flat, forded the low but surprisingly rapid stream, and found a slim walking path into the woods. He secured the reins to a tree, patted his horse and gave her a handful of grain, and began down the path.

The path took a serpentine course, and the trees grew thickly enough that, despite their unleaving, they quickly engulfed him. Lionel strolled along until he could barely hear the ripple of the stream. He saw a broad, flat tree stump that a woodsman had left beside the path. The trees opened above just at that spot, and a wash of silvery light dropped over it. There he sat down with a sigh.

Lionel intended to let his thoughts drift, but before long, without conscious intervention, they were shaping themselves into a prayer.

From what Lionel could tell, he prayed more often than his fellows: prayer seemed to him a natural course of his own mind. While other knights might pray the rosary, as they had all learned in childhood, or what they could remember of psalms, or they might repeat parts of the liturgy they recalled from mass before or after battle, his own prayers would more often follow his thoughts and take shape accordingly as he felt the desire to praise or the need to express the trouble of concern. He didn't know if such practice constituted a sin or even heresy, but he had always believed deep in his own heart that God would hear the private prayer as easily as He would the public.

As he sat on the tree stump, Lionel prayed first for his wife and for the son who had never drawn mortal breath. He felt tears rising, and he let them come, and let them fall, and he felt no less a man as they wetted his clasped hands. He prayed then for his fellows who had fallen battling the Duke of Metz and for those friends with whom he had defended Norman England's northern border. He prayed for his parents and siblings, he prayed thanks for his own healing and for the beauty of autumn and early winter days in his uncle's lands. Then the prayer took its own course, taking from him no conscious direction.

What must I do, then? his prayer asked. What should I do? How should I live? I have lost so much. But I have taken up the knight's calling. How must I perform it, how may I continue?

Have courage, find peace, practice prayer, live with dignity: that answer came to him. He heard it as if it rose from his own thoughts, but he felt as if it had come from elsewhere. He dared not think that God had spoken to him, had answered the prayer for him.

Perhaps God does not answer such prayers, he wondered. Our duty lies in devotion, and answers come in actions, not in words.

Why do you pray so? his thoughts asked. *Do you fear your own death?*

He searched his heart for an answer to that question. No, he thought, I do not fear it. I do not seek it, but I must feel ready when it comes: a knight's duty to himself, to his lord, to God. When it comes, I hope I will face it well, without fear or malice. But I am young and strong: I should live for many years.

For what? a voice deep down asked him—again he wasn't sure if the voice had come from him or not.

He noticed that the light had faded, and the wood was growing dark. Back along the path he thought he saw a figure walking toward him: a young woman in a blue gown. Millicent! No, that could not be true. He shook his head, looked again, and saw nothing. The image had come from his heart, no more.

Lionel followed the path back to his horse, mounted, and began the ride home.

Dusk was spreading, and a bank of slate-grey clouds had scudded in behind the north wind, which also was growing. The moon had already disappeared behind gathering clouds, and the purple horizon to the west had barely held its ground. A light drizzle of sleety rain had begun.

He crested the rise above the wood, and the ground there was already feeling slick, so Lionel turned to the southwest just below the rolling hills. He passed south of the Nahe, but a frosty mist that must have risen from its tumbling waters blew over him. Wrong day to have ridden so far and to have gone so far east, he thought. His blood felt chill, slow in his veins.

Ahead he saw a canopy of trees with a riding path, so he quickened the horse's pace to get a break from the growing cold.

The wide, tree-lined path served almost as an enclosure. The ground felt firm, and the rain stopped: Lionel felt better immediately. He almost wished for a jousting partner: the land there would be perfect for it, and he could use some brisk exercise.

He kept his horse at a canter until he had cleared the trees. To the west, and also looking north, he saw hints of clear sky yet, and the thought of a fire in the great hearth and hot soup and roast meat cheered him. With a little good fortune, and if he judged the land aright in the dark, he should get back in no more than an hour.

My uncle has treated me well, he thought: he ransomed me quickly and has allowed me few duties during my recovery. But I should like to return to England again to see Father and Mother: Mother always knows the right things to say to relieve sorrow and care.

Ah, there is a path, he thought: yes, I know the one. Following it—northwest it turns, directly—I shall return sooner than I guessed. At the thought of warmth and supper, Lionel's blood began to flow again, and his spirits rose.

Lionel heard something ahead: a slow clop and clod of horse's hooves. Someone had come looking for him, he guessed.

He rode on, and out of the gloom rose the image of horse and rider. As he closed, Lionel could tell it was a young man, a knight, who rode directly toward him.

He called out in the local German language, and the rider stopped, but did not reply.

Lionel tried again, the second time in Anglo-Norman, but the rider neither spoke nor resumed his course. He sat still and waited.

Lionel called a third time, trying what he could of the northern French that people spoke across the Disputed Lands to the South. The rider waved to him and began slowly to approach.

Finally Lionel got near enough that he could see a young knight dressed in armor; he had his helmet off and a wool cap on his head and pulled down over his ears so that just a small sweep of blond hair showed beneath. On his shield, hung over the saddle, Lionel observed the device of the soldiers under the Duke of Metz. The armor, Lionel noted, could use a good cleaning.

The knight stopped again—he must have seen the Count Guillaume's device on Lionel's shield.

In the best attempt at the Metzian French that he could manage, Lionel called out, "*Sir, I would speak with you to learn where you are riding and what brings you here.*" He had but two months' experience of the dialect and doubted he had got it entirely right.

The man pulled the hat from his head, tilted his head to one side and then shook it, as if he failed to understand.

Lionel spoke again, this time mustering such Latin as he could. "*Sir, I wish to know where you are riding. The weather is getting poor ahead, and the night has come upon us. If I see correctly, you ally with the knights of Lorraine.*"

The reply came in similarly halting Latin. "*Sir, was that the Metzian dialect you spoke before?*"

"*Perhaps I spoke it poorly.*"

"*You might speak it poorly and still do rather better than I. Have you the gift of many tongues?*"

"*Not such as one may wish. My own comes from Normandy.*"

"*If I speak in the tongue of the south, can you understand me? Soon my Latin will fail me.*"

"*Yes, I think so. I had compeers from the south during my time in England and learned their words also. By now my own town may be more rightly called Anglo-Norman.*"

"Then you have had the gift of many travels, too," the young man replied in southern French, but not quite of the *langue d'oc.* "I am called Sir Alain of the Fair Sands. I come from far to the south to serve my grand kinsman of Lorraine, the Duke of Metz. My mother is elder sister to his wife. I am a young knight, but I bear my title proudly. May I ask your name, sir, and your lord?"

"Sir, I am Sir Lionel, son of Count Robert of Normandy, now knight of Count Guillaume of the Rheinland and Saarland. Today I have ridden out merely for pleasure."

"Then we may not prove so happy to have met each other on this cold night under the clouds. If I may ask one more question, sir, how did you acquire the language of Metz?"

"I had the fortune to enjoy the Duke's hospitality for some two months. That has now been two months ago, and tongues fade when the speaker does not use them."

"You consider your time there a *good* fortune?"

"I would have preferred better fortune, but will make no complaints about my treatment. I was taken in battle not far from here, an hour maybe to the south and west. The Duke's people housed me comfortably, tended my wounds, fed me, brought me books to read, allowed me to hear Sunday mass, and accepted my uncle's ransom-bid for me."

"Ah, Count Guillaume is your uncle. I am glad the Duke showed you good hospitality. I would wish your uncle had shown me the same. You see, I, too, was a casualty of that battle, and I have spent these four months in a cell in the Count's castle."

"May I ride closer?" Lionel asked. "I would know if we have encountered each other on the field."

"Yes, but I do not believe you will be able to tell for sure. I would have no way to recognize your face, nor, I suspect, would you mine. Your carriage on horseback looks unfamiliar to me. If you would ride a few moments with me back in the direction from which I came, there lies a shelter that looks like an abandoned hermitage, and there we may dismount, make a fire, and talk." Sir Alain tugged the wool cap back onto his head.

"Yes, I know the place." Lionel followed Sir Alain, and in no time they found the shelter, tethered their horses, removed their head-gear, and started a small fire in an open flame pit.

"You ride for pleasure always in full armor, Sir Lionel?"

"No: I have just done so in the last few days, intending to get myself back in training. I did not expect to find another knight out riding, especially a foreign knight."

"But look," Alain said, "the moon has come out: I did not imagine the clouds would break this night."

"Stay but an hour, the locals say, and the weather here will change."

Alain examined Lionel's face. "No, I don't believe I have ever seen your face, though I wouldn't have on the battlefield. You have lived for some time with your uncle? I guess, then, that you do not visit his dungeons."

"I have had no occasion. I have been healing from my own griefs—from my own injuries. A sword injury has proven slow to heal."

"I have had one, too, here on my right side."

"And I one on my left."

The knights spoke for a time about the battle four months past and finally agreed that they could not have fought each other, their accounts of the melée being so different.

"But you first said *griefs* before you amended to *injury*," Alain said. "If speaking to a fellow soldier will help, I beg that you tell me your grief."

Lionel knelt to stir the fire.

"I returned to these lands the day after my wife died in childbearing. I should have greeted a wife and son, but found death instead."

"Ah, that is grief indeed! I wish that God may heal you of it!"

"Not in this life, I think," said Lionel, "but in the next."

"I was to be married tonight," Alain said, "to the kindest and loveliest girl I have ever seen. Is it not Christmas Eve?"

"Why, yes, I believe it is—I had lost count of the days. But you will come late to your own wedding. Where was it to take place?"

"In Metz."

"Then you were also riding in the wrong direction."

"Ach, could I have taken the wrong fork? The path divides some half-mile back."

"It does, and you have turned east instead of south.

"The sky had got so dark that I lost my bearings."

"You did not receive such good treatment from my lord as I did from yours," Lionel said. "I am sorry for it. I trust that at least your wound has healed."

"Well enough."

"Have you eaten? I have some food in my saddle-pouch, I think, that I would gladly share. I took some for my ride, but have not used it."

"I would be grateful for it," Alain answered.

"Here, we can warm it at the fire."

The two knights ate together for a few minutes in silence: some roasted meat strips, a few dried fruits and root vegetables, and some bread softened with butter.

"Perchance we two are enemies," Alain said, "though you do not seem to me an enemy, Sir Lionel. The man who released me, your uncle's seneschal, I think, said that on my way departing Count Guillaume's territories I must be ready to fight with any knight of the Count's whom I encountered. He suggested that, given the Duke's recent activities, a knight might insist on it."

"Ah, that was old Sir Charles. Did he say that indeed?"

"I say so not because I have any desire for battle, but for the sake of truth. I have a great hatred of a lie, and saying nothing to you felt to me somehow akin to a lie."

"Did he say *fight* or *joust*?"

"I don't recall, and I may not have understood him aright: he had little French or Latin."

"Grumpy old Sir Charles: his own language comes from the old Franconian—I believe now they call it *Dutch*. I have learned only a very little of it, though he communicates with the Count well enough."

"If indeed he said *joust—alors*, as you can see, I have no spear for jousting. I do bear a sword."

"He can hardly have expected you to fight: he clearly had no one take care of your armor during your . . . time here."

"It is a little dirty, but good enough—not damaged in any way, beyond a dent or two from the day of our mutual skirmish."

"I did not ride seeking battle today, though my armor may suggest otherwise. Yet I would not disappoint my uncle or you, if the order of the day calls for it. Perchance I have brought two spears with me today."

"So I see. As I am, I would not seek a battle, but also as I am, I will not shun one, if the occasion calls for it. Then again, night has fallen fully now, and we have eaten together like friends. And I shall reach my wedding all the later for any delay. And we may do no more than embarrass ourselves: the ground is frosting, so that even a horse may slip."

"Yet the moon is out now, and nearly full. If you have an unhealed injury to your right side, you may not feel ready to fight with a sword. But if you can carry a spear comfortably, we may joust: only a joust, and we have both done our duty. I will lend you a spear gladly. What think you?"

"If you wish it, I will not disappoint you," Sir Alain said.

"I will not go so far as to say I wish it, but we may both excuse ourselves from sloth by saying that the situation calls for it. Let us arm—please choose which of the spears you will. We should test the ground for a good spot. We have sufficient light for a short approach if not a long one."

"Good spears both," Alain said. "I judge them as equals."

"Thank you," Lionel replied. "I made them myself, down to the refining of the points—a hobby I acquired in England during long days waiting for something to happy at the Roman Wall."

The two knights helped each other secure their armor. Lionel felt sad at the condition of his opponent's accoutrements: the Duke's servants had cleaned and repaired his armor during his captivity, but no one had taken the least care with Sir Alain's.

"Your helmet has sustained some damage," Lionel said. "I should have known so when I saw you riding in a cap."

"I wore the cap for warmth. The damage is minimal and the helm sufficient. But thank you for your care."

"Do let me just test this joint here at the shoulder, too, to make it secure. Right: it will keep you safer now. As the foreign knight, Sir Alain, you may choose the side from which you will attack, and you must call the charge."

"I hardly know which side. I will defend the west, then, as nearer to the path that leads south to my home."

The moon shone clearly again and high in the sky.

"Very good. Let us take our places. I will wait to hear your call to charge."

Sir Lionel retreated two score yards east along the path—he could just see Alain, a shadow along the path. He crossed himself and prayed in whispering Latin: *Let me neither cause nor receive more harm than I must.*

Make me the instrument of your peace, Lord—the words came to Lionel's mind, and he wondered if even in a joust he was taking unfair advantage of his opponent. But then he heard Sir Alain's call and the sound of hooves, and he spurred his horse forward, spear in rest.

They had chosen good, flat ground, but the horses advanced with no more than moderate speed: the ground had grown slick, riding path as well as the surrounding grass.

In darkness, however leavened by the brightness of the moon, neither knight had quite prepared for the shock of a spear. Both had taken a short approach, and neither had properly gripped his shield. Lionel's spear struck Alain's shield straight on and burst shards from it. Alain's spear struck Lionel's shield a glancing blow downward and pushed it back hard against his left side.

Both horses reared up, complaining of the abrupt stop to their labor in the dark, and the two knights backed away from each other. Lionel felt a tear in his left side. It felt warm, almost wet, and the pain was sharp.

Alain cantered up to Lionel. "My spear has broken, and you have nearly thrown me. I can joust no more. I fear that makes you the winner, Sir Lionel."

"With neither of us unhorsed, we can declare no winner. We must conclude, unless you would take a chance with your sword, Sir Alain. I trust you received no injury?"

"No, sir, though you struck a fine blow to my shield and have splintered it. I had the oddest feeling that something pushed me back onto my saddle. Otherwise, you would have knocked me from my horse—then we should have had no dispute about the winner."

"Let us dismount, then, and swing our swords a time or two in the name of sport."

"As you wish, sir. I must warn you, though, that I have a particularly fine sword. I was surprised that your lord's seneschal returned it to me. He must not have looked at it closely. At a quick glance, it does not look like much."

"Ah, I have always taken an interest in metal smithing. May I see it?"

The two knights dismounted and tied their horses at the hermitage. Alain drew his sword and handed it pommel first to Lionel.

"I see immediately what you mean. I suspect it is not much to look at even in the light of day, yet it has perfect balance and swings with ease. The leather feels tacky, and, ah, it almost swings itself as one makes the through or downward cut. A marvel of workmanship! I feel glad that Sir Charles at least returned it to you, if not showing it the respect he should have." Lionel handed the pommel back to Alain.

"Thank you! You have many talents and much knowledge, Sir Lionel. May I see your sword as well?"

"I fear that as a weapon it will not impress you, but it has great value to me. My father gave it to me on my sixteenth birthday. You will find it better for beauty than for weaponcraft."

Re-sheathing his own sword, Alain took Lionel's to examine it. "Indeed the smith has made it beautifully. It is a fine sword."

"I have seen many far superior to it and have even used some. But to this one I have become attached, so I may do better with it than I might with a finer weapon."

"Shall we see what we can do, then? I am beginning to believe that morning will rise before we have finished here."

"Quite so. Shall we return to the path where the ground is flat?"

Alain returned the sword and, when they reached their place, drew his own, and Lionel retreated two paces and nodded his head to his opponent.

With no more ado, the two engaged their swords. Both parried well, and the sound of clanging metal resounded through the night.

With three or four passes, Lionel could already tell that Alain had the far superior sword. He must make up the difference with strength and quickness.

Lionel made the first hit: he slipped Alain's sword and struck a blow to the left shoulder. Alain staggered back and nearly fell. Lionel paused.

"Sir Lionel, you have done yourself more harm than good in the repair you made to my armor. I believe you have saved me an injury. But let me see if I cannot return the blow."

They fought again, matching blow for blow, block and parry, cut and thrust. Young men, full of energy and the vigor of youth, will often expend more in sport than they ought. The desire for victory grows beneath the surface of thought, and the heart and muscles, untempered by prudence, will pursue the opponent with deadly commitment even without intention.

Neither man noticed that the moon had nearly disappeared again behind an incoming cloud bank, and they were fighting in conditions as near to dark as still allowed any sight at all.

With an upward stroke aimed to knock the weapon from the opponent's hand, Alain swung toward Lionel with perfect aim and speed. Lionel parried just in time, but the blow drove him upward off his feet. He fell, spun in a circle, and landed firmly on his feet. Locking on his opponent again, he saw that Alain stood with his sword poised above his head. Then he lowered it without striking another blow and backed away.

"You need not have stopped, Sir. I am perfectly healthy."

He did not notice that blood had begun dripping from beneath his armor. The droplets were invisible in the darkness.

"Sir, forgive me, but you will believe I speak either in jest or to gain unfair advantage."

"Speak, please. Having fought with you, I will believe you as I would a brother."

"Well, then, against the better judgment of my mind, my senses tell me that I saw someone on the path just behind you. She stood so close that, when you spun around, I thought you must land right next to her. If she stood there still, she should be standing beside you now."

"She? What could you have seen?"

"I see no one now. But I felt sure I saw—you will not believe me—a maiden, or a young woman. She wore a blue dress and cap, and blonde hair fell around her shoulders. I could see her only because a golden light seemed to me to shine about her."

"Millicent! Can it be? I thought I saw her earlier in the woods some distance east of here. But she has . . ."

"Ach, sir: she was . . ."

"My wife. Truly, I hardly got to know her, but I loved her dearly. The woman you saw, had she . . ."

"Blue eyes? Blue like the clear summer sky?"

"Yes! But how could you see that in the dark? Ah, you must have seen her at the castle during your imprisonment!"

"I assure you as I would a brother, I saw no women there in the castle. They allowed me to see no one but my jailer and the seneschal. I had nearly gone mad for company. As I am a knight, sir, I tell you truly. I held my sword stroke only out of astonishment."

Lionel looked back along the path to the east. "Can spirits, the spirits of the good and just and loving, walk the earth, Sir Alain? And if they can, why will they do so? Should not my loving wife be looking on the face of God, not following the sorrowful days of a husband whose child killed her?"

"Sir Lionel, you have judged yourself too harshly. I feel sorry now that I said anything—I spoke purely out of surprise. Of spiritual matters I know nothing. I have taken my instruction in the Church. I attend mass, and I pray as the priests teach me. Of love I know a little. Of spirits and their path I know nothing."

Lionel felt faint for a moment and heard a buzzing around his ears. Why would Millicent have come? Did she intend to warn me, to encourage me, to stay my hand, to defend me?

"Sir Alain, if indeed you saw the spirit of my wife, if indeed we both did, I would not have her see me pause now that you have struck the better blow. Will you have one more do with me, in her honor?"

"If you wish it, I will, though you have perhaps already done better than you know. I have not fought many battles, but I have never practiced or fought with a swifter and more nimble swordsman."

Lionel again bowed his head to Alain, and with each man poised and ready, they began their bout anew.

After many quick and fervent strokes, Alain swept a horizontal cut directly at Lionel's head.

He ducked just in time, and, slipping beneath and twisting, reversed his sword and swung it directly into

Alain's right side, knocking him from his feet and flat on the ground.

Again Lionel felt a searing pain in his left side, and as the furor of battle subsided, his head began to spin. He shook it repeatedly to regain his senses, then, seeing his opponent stretched on the ground, he threw off his helmet and dashed to his side.

Alain lay semi-conscious, breathing rapidly in short breaths. Lionel's sword blow had dented the knight's armor, but had not fully pierced it. He must have struck the old wound, which had perhaps been worse than Alain had admitted. Lionel gently removed his opponent's helmet and grasped his hand. Alain opened his eyes, and they gradually gained focus.

"Now you have surely won, Sir Lionel. Fine swordplay, from one who knows how to value it. I had not thought to die this day."

"Nor I to kill. We should have stopped: a joust would have been enough."

"But we did not. So go the follies of young men such as we are."

"You need not die, Alain: I can yet get you back to the castle and have your wound tended."

"So that I may again lie in the dungeon, dreaming that I may yet return for my wedding—no, sir, though I thank you. I should then again one day gain release and again face one of the Count's men, but one with not so good a heart. A man could not wish to die at the hand of a more honorable opponent. Look: the snow has begun to fall."

Alain's head flopped to one side. Lionel propped it with a glove to keep it from the cold ground. He could see snowflakes fall and die across the breast of Alain's armor.

"I fear, my friend, that you may not outlive me by much." Alain pointed at the ground by Lionel's side. There grew a pool of dark blood, dripping from beneath Lionel's armor. "I believe, sir, that you are a man of God as well as a soldier. Please pray for my soul that the angels may take me. I have never been a bad man, though I have not prayed as much as I could have. Please pray also for my Élise: she should have been my bride. Speech fails me. I free you of my death: I know you did not intend it. Please pray for . . ." Alain's voice fell silent.

Lionel's forehead felt hot with fever, and the tears in his eyes evaporated as they touched his cheek. He lay his forehead on the cold metal of Alain's breast-armor. *May the angels take your soul, Sir Alain*, he prayed, *and may my Millicent greet you at the Gate of Heaven and beg forgiveness for me even as she leads you in.*

Lionel felt that in a minute or a little more he, too, must die.

He felt a hand touch him from behind, but he had no strength to turn to see to whom it belonged—a soft hand, a woman's hand. It felt warm, and the warmth passed through him to the wound in his side. And the pain eased. And he felt his breath strengthen.

Millicent, he thought, and he smiled.

For a minute, he felt as though he had tumbled from consciousness into sleep. He lay with his back on the ground, and as he looked up, he saw Millicent and Alain standing beside him, both smiling at him. Then the image of Alain began to fade.

That must not happen, Lionel thought. Élise, yes that was the name he spoke, will be needing him. She must not go on alone. Lionel fought to wake.

He found himself alone on the cold ground save the breathless body of Sir Alain, snowflakes dotting his face and gradually covering the ground. He rolled over and placed his hand over the heart of the fallen knight.

"Millicent, if your spirit has returned to this earth to save me, I must use such power as you have given me to save this good young man."

He prayed, pouring out his heart in his own native tongue.

"Lord, until this day I have never prayed to ask you for anything. I have prayed that your angels may take the soul of the knight I have unwillingly killed. To think that we have fought so for sport! Ah, what we young men think, and what we do! Now I pray you with all my heart, and through the loving heart of my saint, Millicent, who touches me with your love, to take whatever power keeps me alive and bestow it on the body of Sir Alain. He must have his wife and know her love, as I have had wife and love. If ever a poor young man's voice may touch Almighty Spirit, please save this knight, and take me in his place. I will ask no more of you in this life, and I will ask only one thing in the next."

Lionel scrambled to his knees. He put Alain's sword on his breast, the pommel resting just shy of his chin, and crossed the young man's hands over top of it. He turned the head so that it faced directly up toward the heavens.

Again he touched the armor over Alain's heart, and he lay his head on Alain's side, where he determined the injury must be. He thought he saw a hint of light in the eastern sky, and then he closed his eyes.

I will see you soon, Millicent, if I am good enough, Lionel thought. If God grants prayers in death and in life, and if I have lived well enough to deserve his Grace and you, we will not again be parted. For now I must sleep.

***

Sleep fell upon Lionel like a fog, and he felt as though his body were whirling in the air. I am not sleeping, he thought, but dying.

Not yet, a voice said to him. He looked up and raised a hand toward the voice.

I do not mind. I have tried to live, while I lived, the life of a good man.

You have, the voice said.

Who are you? Lionel asked.

You know who I am.

Dare I believe it?

No need to dare.

Two blue eyes looked down into his through the roiling fog. You have a wound, the voice said. Let me heal it.

A warm, soft hand touched the wound as though Lionel were wearing no armor at all. The pain immediately dispersed, and the wound began to close.

Wait! Lionel said. If you heal me, this man will die. I have lost you. Shall his love lose him, too? You must let me take the warmth in my hands: I may yet save him!

Then your own life will end.

It will not end. It will begin again, God willing. I will find you there.

Only God can tell, not I.

Place the warmth in my hands, I beg you.

Between waking and sleeping, Lionel turned and placed his right hand on Sir Alain's side where the wound must be. Then he lay his head down over the man's heart.

Make me an instrument of your peace.

He thought he heard, beating just beneath his ear, the heart of the opponent he had with no malice felled.

Ah.

Lionel had no more strength to rise, but even as the cold began to steal through his veins, he felt a new warmth, as if someone had covered him with a cloak.

You have done well, my love, the soft voice said, and Lionel felt his consciousness slip away as the blood had from his body.

***

Alain began to wake out of deep pit of darkness. He felt no pain, but instead a weight upon his breast. He propped himself up on his hands, then turned over the body of Sir Lionel. The face was smiling, and while the rest of the body looked to be freezing, the right hand felt warm. A cloak had fallen alongside the body on the path. He took it and draped it over the cold corpse of the knight.

***

Sir Albert, still riding as he had through the night, had come to a fork in the road. As he was about to turn left, to the north and west, guessing that he must ride that way to plead the ransom of his brother from the Count Guillaume, he saw a sudden burst of light along the right-hand path to the east. He rode that way. The ground bore a dusting of frost and snow.

A short way down the path, he found two knights, one sitting part way up with his back to Albert, propped on his hands, and the other lying with his head in the first knight's lap. The armor of the first man looked like that of the soldiers of the Duke of Metz.

"Sir," he called out, "has some mishap befallen you, and do you need assistance?"

Alain turned his head as far as he could. "I am well enough, I think, but my companion is dead. Your voice, sir, rings familiar. I am Alain, knight of the Duke of Metz."

"Alain, beyond hope I have found you! I am Albert, your brother!"

"You have found me, but not beyond hope. And I thank you and God for it. Albert, I am very glad to see you. But why have you come?"

"To look for you! You were to have married the Lady Élise yesterday. When you had not returned, I asked the Duke for permission to search for you. He would permit no others to come, but he did allow me. I thought to search as far as the Count Guillaume's castle if I needed to, and I determined not to return without you, or at least word of you and your health."

"A man could not ask for a finer brother. And as for this man here with me, I could not have asked for a finer friend—nor a better spiritual teacher."

Albert jumped down from his horse and went to his brother's side. "He looks like one of Count Guillaume's knights."

"He was."

"How did he die? Did you find him lying here?"

"I killed him."

"You killed him? But his face: he looks to be smiling."

"Yes, I know. That is why I haven't risen."

"Can you stand?"

"I think so. Will you give me a hand, please?

Albert helped Alain rise to his feet. "You seem sturdy enough to me, brother."

Alain too the blue cloak and placed it beneath Lionel's head.

"Yes, and that is another odd thing. You see, last night, or rather probably just an hour or two ago, this knight, Sir Lionel was his name, killed me."

"He killed you? Have you gone mad, Alain?"

"Perhaps, but I do not think so. Let me tell you what happened."

"I would rejoice to hear, but first listen to a brother's advice. We are both in unfriendly lands. If I have my way, we will ride south and pass the Disputed Lands before we take time for conversation. Don't forget that Lady Élise and our parents await your return. I would hate to lose you again now that I have found you."

"Count Guillaume has released me."

"And you have killed one of his knights."

"Before we go, we must do something to honor the body of this noble man. I owe him and God a great debt and would do nothing offensive to either."

"I understand you partly, but we can hardly bury him or take his body to the Count."

"Just over there we will find an abandoned hermitage. We may lay the body there with honors."

"Where did this blue cloth come from? It looks like a lady's cloak."

"I will explain that, too."

The brothers carried Lionel's body to the hermitage. They wrapped it as well as they could in the blue cloak. The face still shone with a gentle smile. Sir Alain knelt and prayed over the body, and he asked that his brother do the same.

Alain found a wooden tablet and some charcoal in a corner of the hermitage, and on the tablet he wrote this inscription in halting Latin:

In yon hermitage a short distance along the eastward path lie the mortal remains of Sir Lionel, knight to Count Guillaume of Rheinland-Saarland and to God, who watches over all. He died to save the life of a fellow knight whom he met in a sporting encounter and whom he defeated. He died of an old wound. That knight will honor him, and he will honor God, all the days of his life. May the angels bless him as he so well deserves, and may he find his beloved Lady Millicent on the shores of Heaven.

When Albert believed they could not safely wait a minute longer, he persuaded Alain to mount. Alain carried with him his opponent's sword and helmet. They rode for the crossroad, and before they turned south, Sir Alain thrust Lionel's sword in the ground right where the paths crossed—it passed into the ground easily despite the frost and snow. He placed Sir Lionel's helmet and the tablet leaning against the sword. He crossed himself, uttered a final prayer, and nodded to his brother. Then the two French knights rode south, keeping a steady pace along the path for some hours until they reached the Disputed Lands, passed through them, and greeted beyond a party of Metzian knights who would see them on home.

As they rode, Alain told his brother the story of his encounter with Lionel and with death. He recounted the details of how they had met, what had happened in their bout, and how, with the hand of Sir Lionel upon his heart, he had passed into darkness and revived again.

Just after full sunrise and no more than minutes after Alain and Albert had ridden away, a small party of Count Guillaume's knights came riding south from the castle: they were searching for Sir Lionel, who had not returned from his ride. When they reached the crossroad, they found Lionel's sword and helm and the inscribed tablet that Sir Alain had left with them. They rode on to the hermitage and found the body, wrapped in the blue cloak.

"What should we do?" one of them asked.

"We should pursue the man who left the note," said the second.

"Which way?" said the third.

"South, toward the border," answered the second. "I suspect the Metzians, despite their promise of peace. And we have never got proper vengeance."

"Who knows how long a start they have had," said the first.

The fourth had remained beside the body, kneeling. "Look at his face! The smile! I have seen dead men, but have never seen a face look so composed, so peaceful—so happy. I have seldom seen such a look on living faces!"

The others gathered round.

The third knight spoke. "First, I think we should take the body back to the castle. This man has suffered more than his share of grief, and now he has left this sad world behind.

Let us take him back and honor his life and death such as we may."

"Where do you suppose the cloak came from?" asked the first.

"That I can answer," said the fourth. "It came from an angel."

The others laughed, though more out of sympathy than humor.

The fourth knight did not laugh.

"A fine Christmas gift," said the second knight, "for the Count: the dead body of his nephew. We shall be sent riding south, I suspect."

"Was he indeed the Count's nephew?" asked the second knight.

"His wife, I recall, Lady Millicent, always dressed in blue. From what I knew of him, Sir Lionel was a good man and a gift to his uncle while he lived. He has now, I believe, made a gift of his soul, returning it to God."

"We should get back to the castle in time for Christmas breakfast," said the first knight.

"We should get a litter to transport the body," said the second.

"You go ahead," said the fourth. "I'll keep watch until you return, and I will tend his horse."

He stood and watched as the other three horsemen rode west and then turned north, out of view. The land there flowed in low, rolling hills rising gently toward the castle in the distance. The morning air still felt cold, but the sun was beginning to turn the frost and remaining snow into silver rivulets that would trickle south and obscure the hoofprints on the path. Something marvelous about the face, he thought, and he went over to the horse, who nickered with hunger.

***

In times to come Sir Alain and Lady Élise name their daughter Millicent and their son Lionel.

A WALK IN THE DARK

Freawaru's Lament

(from Algar's Stories from Beowulf, 2012)

UP THIS RISE, YET, TO THE BURH, BROTHER OSWALT thought. Snow had begun to fall, but the true cold of winter hadn't yet settled into the North.

You will find her there, he thought he heard a voice say, but he saw no one anywhere near.

He hoped to find the old storyteller of whom he had heard so much and for whom he had been searching. As he climbed, he noticed someone had opened the gate.

***

Generations after the events that she narrated, she sat by the hearth, the old woman, *völva* some called her in the northlands, *prophetess* said others, *sibyl* in the old language of the far south. Probably she was just someone who liked to tell stories to her grandchildren, stories especially that called back to mind her ancestors and how they had won glory or suffered sorrows, to remind the young that life is hard, as they must soon enough learn for themselves.

She sat in the midst of the children, petting the hair of a lovely granddaughter who always sat wide-eyed, her lips slightly parted in awe, as her "beppe" wove magic with words, built syllables into shadows that peopled the long evenings with heroes and heroines, villains and monsters, and more often than not just plain folk who teetered their way through obstacles of tragedy and horror. Intoning deeply, with steady measure she chanted by tepid lamplight a favorite old story, a fragment, rebuilding, creating, something between fact and memory. She told her grandmother's tale, but after the fashion it was given her by the cold wind singing off the glacier and riding back up the fjord over frantic, giving, unforgiving waves.

In a corner, under a brighter light but out of the way, a scribe, the young monk in a dark cowl, born and bred a Christian far away, detachedly scribbled in a crabbed but quick hand the tale he heard from that local prophet. He resisted, when he could, the temptation to edit or to add or to get caught up himself in the feel of the tale or to find himself in it and sympathize too greatly with this one or that one and thus lose its course or details—a hard job, that, since we make tales so that in them we may lose ourselves, then find ourselves anew thereafter.

And so she sang, closing her eyes tightly, without even a lyre to strum in accompaniment, but with the gentle drumming of a grandson's hand upon the table where he sat echoing the rhythms as distant thunder does a waking heartbeat.

> "Only a child I was handed over
> to Ingeld the Heathobard, who raised a great hall,
> son of Froda, the father now slain
> and son put to flight, fled from his bride
> who now belongs to two folk and none.
> Like my proud mother, I the price paid
> to cool the blood-feud, end the choler,
> but all men know, as the hero foretold,
> he who slew Grendel and Grendel's dam,
> that anger abides among soldiers, old and young:
> 'seldom sleeps death-spear, though the bride abide
> in the hearts of the people as kind and good,
> nobly attending and pouring fine ale,
> for betimes it happens a family heirloom
> shines on the belt of one once enemy,
> and the old one sees it, scarred and ornery,
> ancient ash-warrior, tells in his wrath
> the untamed youth too quick to vengeance,

tells him his ancestor wore that weapon,
cut down in battle by this foe now friend.
Swift again then the action or arm,
and the shadow of shields, steel and linden.
So it goes among soldiers and dragons,
through these regions rife with revenge,
unwary of war when glory looms lovely'—
lovelier than the faces of wives and daughters
who pray for peace and play at weaving it.
Now he hides from the Danes my brothers,
improves his strength and rebuilds his army,
he who wed me to wash war from our peoples,
Ingeld, who could not keep his hand from the sword
or his heart from a new crown, though it be not his
by right or fortune, but God's gift to the Danes,
and he as I thought once good husband and true,
true still, as I'm told, though far from my eyes."

Thus sang the queen, callow and slender,
quiet by habit and kind in her glance,
but already weary, not long for a world
filled largely with sorrow. *Freawaru* they called her,
'nobly attentive,' or 'ladylike aspect,'
or sometimes *Hrut*, at first a pet-name
from her father Hrothgar, first meaning 'sheep,'
later an insult, less than courtly,
mumbled by soldiers who saw her shipped off
to an enemy to end their conflict, less than sure
of the wisdom of sending one so beautiful

to become a betrayer to him who would end
a parlay only with blood—damned be the peacemaker
when sword should decide, they said aside.

What else for her but lament, the fine lady,
hardly more than a girl, from whom hopeful parents
expected so much (impossible, I'd say),
unbeguiled loyalty from two lordly kin
long at feud and short on forgiveness?
Leaving   home   with   heart-pang,   parting   from
parents,
to live among foreigners far from her family,
perhaps well-loved, perhaps a slave
or little better, honored or lost,
long-lived among nobles, or outcast unwanted,
graced in her children, or dead upon child-bed.
One fate for certain for faithful Freawaru,
as it shall be for all: our portion of suffering.

Likewise had life gone for hardy Hildeburh,
daughter of Hoc, sister of Hnaef
who gave his life to retrieve his sister
when Finn's folk betrayed them.
Finn of the Eotens, giants among men,
married Hoc's daughter to mend his feud
with the half-Danes. Death comes to all
tribes, that much we know truly,
and when Hnaef came to comfort his sister
far from her own folk, hostility rose anew

as it tends to do, then and now, too.
Hnaef was slain by an Eoten sword,
by an old one who would not forget a foe;
then nothing could calm that clash. Cold weather
brought truce, but truly in time
the Danes, feigning peace, felled Finn
and his whole house, sailed home sated
with enemy blood, and poor Hildeburh, hardly
more than the age of a maid, made glad
before by her children, belying her youth,
turned nowhere then but to tears and sorrow
by the death of both husband and sons
at the hands of her kinfolk, just though they were
in revenge. Rarely does the peace-weaver's role
last free of heartbreak for a fair hour.
So later it proved for her kinswoman, pining
fitfully for a mate little wiser than Finn
in his failure to cull the wrath of his folk:
Freawaru, she was, Ingeld's bride,
beauty of the Danes."

The old woman paused a moment in her story, swaying gently, quietly humming or moaning, the children couldn't tell which. They felt the break in her story like the seam in a shoe that rubs the foot raw until one stops to adjust it, then continues walking over hills and fields, so that relieved of one pain, one must confront the headwind again, until it too disappears in the wake of the progress and process of thoughts.

The scribe held his pen poised, dared to shake out his wrist just a bit, and looked up half expectantly, half wishing his task soon over. He may have missed a line or two as his mind drifted, until the impelling, elegant chant of the of the gray-haired singer, now resumed, pulled him once more into a world lost somewhere between history and dream, the tale of Freawaru's failed peace mission.

"Betimes in private this message received,
faithful Freawaru from her ill-fated husband,
after months of waiting for unhappy Ingeld,
the anxious princess willingly gave audience
to a runner arrived with rune-staff in hand,
and for this message he had hoped for reward:
"Now alone I may send to you how in a ship
I came here, so you will know how my thoughts
rest only with you: from my heart you will hear
    the truth of our covenant, though the world come between,"
wrote Ingeld, both prince and purveyor of death.
"Heartfelt love I send. Little good it will do you.
I who carve this message in wood recall to your mind
the vows we made together in milder times.
In your hands now lies the life of our son,
the fate of our hall where festive we dwelt
till my heart turned to war: fine friendship that,
to your trusting father and his fair daughter
so young in years, pure in your thoughts.
This I then ask you: guard our son,

Put him in protection of noble Folcwalda my
counselor,
appoint a good guard to yourself and go
to the ship I left you, follow the soldier
who bears this message. Let no one bind you
to other course than to take this voyage
and here, under the cliff's edge, high
off the shore, find the husband who loves you surely,
near the thwaite where the thrush sings in the
thicket.
Follow the current south where a man with few
comrades
may yet win gold with his courage, regain
enough glory to win back his honor and, he hopes,
his wife. So only, that way and no other,
may he assuage the anguish that augers
no rest in his heart. You, royal daughter,
must seek that Angle of land where the bright sun
dies into the whale-road, and so still this worry."

Thus his penitent message; so her measured reply:
'Born to exile, burnt to the spirit
now, once bold in my thoughts to bind peace
between peoples, bade love a husband made plain
just once to my eyes ere our marriage,
and that while he sat high on a horse,
hidden behind helm and heavy with mail,
and now become would-be bane to my brothers—
and yet I do love him, to my lasting sorrow.

And so as my lord commands me, I come,
to find his sanctuary and share privation--
or glory, too, should that come again.
Ill-starred the future for those who scheme murder,
and ill-starred for his child peaceful at home.
Restless the rover who strives to rule kingdoms,
comfortless his love, cold and alone.
We two made a vow; no vengeance may annul it,
and I must bear enmity either way:
from brothers lost to me, distanced by battle
with me, one-flesh wife of their Heathobard foe,
a husband who fears my heart truer to the Danes.
So I weep likewise for brother and bond,
and find small comfort that one weeps for me.
Alone only may the world's exile—
each one of us finally—find joy in the earth,
sewn to sleep with the ground our mother,
or drowned in the dreary sea. Do not dare
expect me, yet ever I seek you,
for your fate with mine is now folded.
And so the son whom together we made
must seek out his own place and time, despite his
parents.
Woe to the one who must ever wait
for love to come reborn out of longing,
or for longing only returned for her love.
So sorrow survives us, a sea of trouble.
I kiss your son and come, my husband,
to find you: may my brothers forgive me.'

So says the sage: let youth stay ever stern
of mind, sturdy of purpose, and he shall sustain
both anxiety and grief. Let him give all he has
to his lord or the poor, and find his pleasure
in silence alone, or in service to his Lord.
Be he outcast or beggar, exile or king,
find he evil companions or stout-hearted friends,
one fate comes to all, and all come to him:
let him live while he can and hope for the best,
never forgetting that fretless labor
and steadfast courage make and sustain a just man—
or a just woman—and those jewels alone
lend us the wages of life till time lowers
us all a last long time
into the wild waves or under the hill.

Let the maid with her mother
find peace among her family,
the youth yearn for no more than his homeland;
let both hope to be matched well in marriage
and to find pleasure in the work life presents them.
And when chance gives choices, for joy or grief,
may they know well the wide world
bestows what it will, belies our wishes,
and for all our questions and quarrels
offers us neither answer nor ease.
Few virtues prove surer than the strength to endure.
So knows the soldier wielding his sword,

and so the farmer pushing his plow."

Her sage or mine? thought the scribe, as he quickly rubbed a cramp from his hand and scratched the dry skin from around his tonsure. She had not paused and seldom even faltered, lost seemingly in her trance or in the glow of attention tale-telling brought her—so, as quickly as he could, he returned to his discipline. Are they so different? he dared to muse. Or have our worlds parted forever? Has God lost this woman, or will he recover her? Why does He permit the passing on of such stories and the joy we find in them? Will He save the children from them, or does He teach through them? Is *our* Lord *her* Lord also as He wends through the world of her waking dreams?

He shook out his thoughts, stretched his eyelids, and returned nose and pen to page, writing the tale he heard told, a tale magic with music.

"Then in fitful prayer poor Freawaru
to a distant Father, dour as she thought,
hurried her tale of hope beyond hope,
chanted an *ave*, choosing words sparely
as she rushed to her ship,
trusting that those men served their master
as she did her husband, that they did not harbor
their own designs in a false dispatch.
Like a fisherman in new-found waters,
eager to cast and angle a catch
to feed his family, so often to fortune

we allow our lot, with no hour to temper
action with reason, the instant demands
we make a choice, and may chance preserve us,
so Freawaru giving her son into Folcwalda's hands
boarded the boat she had to believe
would carry her swiftly to care for her love,
and so she spoke:

'Worthy is she who wears faith in her face
and carries it calm and strong in her heart,
O Father, who fixes minds firmly,
so care and longing lie cast aside;
quiet my fears, may anxiety fade,
and may I find my strength secure in you.
All's well only for the one who seeks grace
in the Lord of Heaven, who lays aside hoards
of treasure for trust in our source and stay:
may wind and current carry as you will!'"

[So spoke the old singer, and her scribe nodded.]

"Like the thane turned wanderer when tide
or sword take his lord, the lady, too,
shorn of her family, but firm of purpose,
may seek solace over the stone-cold sea,
anxious of folly and inexorable fate.
Grief makes a cruel companion, cold
for the wayfarer who has lost close friends;
well she remembers a generous lord, genial

allies arrayed on the mead-benches, ale

freeing the words that wreath the mead-hall

in loving kindness, free those who still lust for revenge."

Faith and fate, thought the scribe, barely catching himself as he almost tumbled into dream of his own: how can she blend them? Has no one taught her better, or does she simply refuse to learn, lost in the old ways? Worse still—he feared even to admit the thought—does she see something beyond what we see, something as ancient and true, as necessary, to which our ears have become deaf and our hearts blind? Again he caught himself and resumed, biting his thumb to focus attention.

But even the taste of his blood could not fully still his own mind, desperate with images. The old woman's words wove themselves in and out of his own imaginings, as Freawaru sailed from place to place, seeking news of her husband, lost to exile and chance and the will of God.

She came then south to the land of the Jutes, or Eotens as they say, that folk who once in the age of Finn and Hildeburh had also warred against the Danes. Now, with the young queen at their mercy, they could have begun their feud anew or simply taken cruel vengeance with no one the wiser. Sometimes time stills rage, and sometimes it does not.

At that time gentle Freawaru found welcome among the Frisian islanders. When their king learned of her plight, he went himself to meet her, and finding himself won by her beauty, devotion, and calm spirit, and believing her mission impossible—for she spoke her history clearly and openly— he offered his own son Caelic, often called Finning by his family, as a husband to her. He doubted, he said, that she could ever find Ingeld among the lands to the south, even if she could reach them, for the lands were many, and knowledge of them in the North piecemeal at best. Truly, pirates harried those lands and the sea and shore alike. Surely she could find happiness with a new and not ignoble folk and bring the old feud, which had never properly ended, to the peaceful conclusion, though Hildeburh could not.

Yet however the king pressed her, Freawaru graciously refused: not so easy to refuse a king, try it who will! She had, she said, but one purpose left to her: keeping faith to her husband and to her father's wishes, and to her peoples' hopes for peace. Perhaps in pursuing her quest, in this life and beyond, if necessary, she could encourage other souls lost to sorrow and exile, both those who sought and those themselves sought by others, waiting in patience and hope for a distant love to find them and release them from pain.

And so with the disappointed blessing of king and prince, Freawaru, comforted barely with a simple meal and some rest and repast for her oarsmen, resumed her journey, seeking, seeking where? seeking why? Who would not shed a tear for Freawaru, yet who could not admire her devotion, such devotion as even a poor monk must admire, himself an exile in the shadow-lands of the North among barely believers and their haunting stories, where a warm loaf of bread and a horn of cool ale offered only occasional hints of home, and no Freawaru to seek him out and make familiar whatever place in which he found himself, his home in her love, her heart his.

Onward she must sail, and onward he, to God knows where, her story as common as weary feet and hands clasped against the cold, on to many lands and little news. *No*, folk answered, none had heard; then *yes*, someone had heard of Ingeld, alive, perhaps, far to the south, hiding, seeking a ship.

Then, easing from his reverie, the scribe felt sure once again that he heard the poet's own words, and he recorded with all the diligence his energy would allow.

> "Where has the steed gone, where the soldier,
> the high-flying hawk and the honer of treasures?
> Where the choice banquets, the shining chalice
> the ancient ale-horn in the hand of a hero?
> where the proud princeling and plated torque
> that adorned the white throat and lit it with gold?
> Where have they gone? groans the voice of the princess,
> lost in the wind-swirls and wretched with cold.
> Comes the snow, or comes the darkness,
> comes the hailstorm holy or damned;
> one thing is general: sooner or later
> we all learn suffering, the loss of a babe,
> the pain of a wound where once on a time

a trusted limb bore a touted sword,
heirloom of heroes, the long-hailed quest
at last failed—how then to go home?
Then must he wander, the aged and weathered one,
last of his people though hardened to peril,
or the exiled spearman, scourge of his race,
or the lordless lad left after battle,
so also the wronged woman, wrested from home
to serve her tribe and tame her husband.
No one finds good fortune forever,
though it last the life long.

"Sometimes when sorrow and sleep come together,
her man embraces her warm in his arms,
and she enjoys again what has become enemy
to her heart: remembrance of hearth and home.
The she wakes, sees spreading over the waves
the wings of sea birds, whirling and diving,
falling like snow. All that rises falls,
all that's born is buried, all sage is sullied,
and all that dares live declines, decays.
What joy in words!"

Not so unlike my own training, this, thought the
scribe, as once more the swaying matron paused in her
chant. Then her eyes opened, and she smiled at the children
who sat beside and around her somewhere amidst sleep and
thraldom and the world that melds history and
imagination. The scribe scratched his head, dipped his pen,

and waited poised, for a long moment, sure that she must not end her tale with longing and irony, sending the children to bed with her sorrow as well as their own. Do children fall asleep in sorrow? He couldn't remember, and the thought disappeared as, smiling, she took up the chant, but moderate in her tone and kind in her demeanor.

> "Fine princess and queen, fair Freawaru,
> Hrut to her father Hrothgar the wise
> of Heorot in Denmark, heart of the north world,
> sought long for her husband, him of the Heathobards.
> And did she find him, stout-hearted friend
> to all whom she loved? No lay tells us,
> but this much I know of princess or thane:
> anger in action brings blood and the ache
> of vengeance, never stilled; verily say the stories,
> and your own heart will hear it, hatred
> begets but hatred alone, and hatred buried
> lies buried not long, but lives again
> like the worm on the willow, soft
> and hidden, but delving and lurking, hardly
> dead, but feeding and growing, gobbling
> up gall like the greed of the dragon
> and spreading it all like the spidery root
> that destroys the foundation of hall or heart.
> Remember Freawaru, her restless devotion.
> Do someone a kindness, and take that to your dreams,
> and good Freawaru, still a-sail, will find you,
> for that is her task in the fullness of time,

to seek out others in sorrow and longing
who despite discomfiture find within them
forgiveness and faithfulness. Her smile will fill you
with gladness and mercy, her mild eyes
grace you with peace and calm sleep.
And if you recall, recite a short prayer
to almighty All-Father for fair Freawaru
who shares good dreams as she sails by.
Remember your loving mother and father, sister
and brother, and the grandmother who tucks you in
bed."

Slowly she rose, straightening her back with difficulty, and eased the sleepy children one by one to their feet and off to their warm beds.

"Beppe," said the one child yet awake enough to ask, "How does the story end?"

"Stories don't end," the grandmother said. "They only stop for sleep."

"But about Freawaru: what really happened to Freawaru?"

"Some say she found Ingeld, and together they traveled to the lands of the east and served in the court of the king of a grand place called Constantinople. Some say she sailed into the mists of the sea and landed in the realm of the elves, where she sang her sad tale and won the hearts of that folk. Some say, as in the lay I sang you, she sails still, into the dreams of children, to calm them for sleep and watch over them. Come now and learn for yourself."

She turned and winked at the scribe when she saw his eyes focused on her. With his cramped hand he wrought the last of the letters recording her tale. "Some say," the old woman whispered, looking at the monk intently, "Freawaru's ghost visits old grandmothers so that we may tell her story to the young—or to curious, wandering monks." She smiled, but the monk had returned his eyes to his script.

Seconds later he nodded back, intending to thank her, but when he raised his eyes, the old storyteller had gone. He blew on the scribbled figures of his page to dry the ink so it wouldn't smudge. He looked around with tired eyes, but the hall was empty.

What of the end of the story? What of Freawaru and Ingeld? What is it with these people, he thought, and their maddening way of escaping endings, so we don't know *what happens*, the finality of joys and sorrows?

What do we make of stories and their endings? Are they any more than pass-time, random fits of imagined adventure? Astray of scripture, he wondered, can they do more harm than good? Where does their power come from? For surely they have power.

The young monk, trained to seek stories and record them, extinguished his lamp and let the dying embers of the hearthfire guide him to the door. He pulled the hood of his cowl tightly over his head and opened the door and pulled on some woolen gloves: he had far to walk that night. Brother Oswalt set his foot to the growing cover of snow and considered the course of his prayers.

Letters from Petrarch

IN EARLY MAY, THE KINDEST MONTH IN FLORENCE, THE air often remains cool, especially in the evening. Breezes pass through the arches in the center of the Ponte Vecchio, and moonlight dashes off the Arno as sunset casts red-gold and purple-blue filigrees over the western sky.

Some critics may call the city touristy, but I love visiting Florence, thought Laura Campanelli, Professor of Comparative Literature, lover of old manuscripts, literature in the blaze of its aesthetic best, and the natural, antique, and contemporary beauties of Italian culture.

As soon as spring term ended, she had caught a plane for Florence, stayed a day strolling in the downtown to recover from jet lag, attended mass at Santa Marie dei Fiori, and then taken a train to Verona, where she visited the cathedral library. There in 1345 Petrarch had found a collection of letters that Cicero had written to his friend Titus Pomponius Atticus between 68 and 44 BC: letters of advice or wisdom or sometimes just simple affection.

As did Petrarch, Laura had always wondered about those letters. She also wondered how someone as sagacious and practiced in statecraft as Cicero could have given thoughtful advice to others over so many years of his life and yet could have got himself into so much trouble. After Caesar's murder, Cicero had supported Octavian against Antony, but when the two men reconciled and agreed to rule together with Lepidus, Antony had Cicero murdered. Not satisfied at that, Antony ordered that Cicero's head and hands be nailed on the wall at the Roman Forum.

In an astonishing and wonderful turn of mind, Petrarch, after his discovery of the letters in Verona, he had not only set himself to preserving the manuscripts, but had also written letters of his own to Cicero, a man who had died almost fourteen hundred years before his time.

An admirer of all things Classical, Petrarch had first found an intellectual hero in Cicero. But as he came to understand the famous orator better, he had come to find the man behind the legend quarrelsome, arrogant, and ambitious.

As far as Laura knew, only two of Petrarch's letters to Cicero had come to light, one of which most scholars have proclaimed spurious. The remaining letter, while deferential and commendatory with respect to Cicero's abilities, chastises him for "opportunism," "fickleness," and "inconsistency." Petrarch, too, failed to appreciate how such a wise man could have forgotten his own best counsel.

For his antiquarian efforts, Petrarch had called himself a "devoted follower of Pallas Athena who got himself entangled in the web of wisdom's enemy, the spider"—finding old manuscripts is only half the battle, since preserving them may prove even harder. Laura recalled the mummified cat in the reliquary at Petrarch's home in Arquà, with its pledge of fidelity carved in stone beneath.

She had loved Petrarch's sonnets since first reading them in undergraduate school—how could she not adore "Laura" poems?—but for a poet to have a poet-cat as well had brought her unqualified glee despite the morbidness of the exhibit. Here is what the cat speaks from the stone:

> "The prophet bore two loves:
> I was the greater fire, Laura the second.
> Why do you laugh? If she had a divine shape,
> In me he had a worthy, faithful love.
> If she engendered many sacred books,
> I am the cause that mice did not eat them!

Protect this sacred boundary from mice,
That they dare not consume my lord's eloquence!
I will frighten them even after my death:
This lasting duty lives in my lifeless body."

Who can fail to love such a cat—and such a lord?
Laura thought.

At a winter academic conference in Boston, Laura had
learned that a former Cambridge professor of manuscript
studies had been following the track of additional Petrarch
letters: he had found traces of their recovery in three
centuries of correspondence among Italian collectors, and,
having got too old to travel comfortably, he had asked Laura
to take up pursuit, guessing that she might be the only
person to enjoy it as much as he or to search with similar
zeal.

The latest of the collectors had supposedly donated
the letters to one of the great libraries, but no one seemed
to know which one, and no available catalogue listed them.

With letters of introduction from her college dean and
from the Cambridge scholar and his Italian colleagues,
Laura had gained permission to re-search the library in
Verona, but had found nothing new—not even traces.
Following the librarian's advice, she had returned to
Florence and searched everything she could lay hands on at
the Biblioteca Medicea—Laurenziana on the Piazza di San
Lorenzo. Even with the help of fully trained and eager
library assistants, she could find nothing.

So after several long days' work, she had reached a standstill in her research. She settled into a B&B north of the downtown and had a quiet dinner at a lovely little place called Trattoria Tito, and then she had strolled down the hill to the river and out along the old bridge.

The streets remained crowded with Florentines as well as tourists even as bridge traffic had begun to thin, and shop keepers were just beginning to turn on their lights. Bulbs blinked on serially or in tandem, hinting of Christmas even in the pleasant May evening air.

Once again she took out the copy of Petrarch's letter than she had hand printed: it had grown wrinkled and worn, but looking at it again by lamplight gave her a sense of comfort and encouraged her to continue the search.

Laura thought she caught a whiff of raw meat, but that couldn't be: centuries had passed since the bridge had housed a row of butchers' shops, and her dinner had settled nicely. Wisps of leather and wool followed, but they too passed—must be the flotsam and jetsam of the Arno, she thought.

Without realizing it, she had begun to read the letter aloud, almost to recite from memory, when she felt a tug at her sleeve.

"*He should have listened,*" a man's voice spoke softly in Italian. It came from a figure of about her height shrouded in a brown Franciscan cloak. The man released her sleeve, but did not turn to face her. He wore the hood over his head despite the relative warmth of the evening.

"*Who should have listened?*" Laura asked, responding in Italian.

"*Cicero,*" the man replied. He spoke the name after Italian rather than Roman phonology, "CHI-chuh-ro." His accent sounded Tuscan, but antiquated. "*You were quoting from his letter to Cicero—Francesco's, that is, Petrarca's.*"

Again the man did not turn his face toward her, but around the edge of the hood Laura could see the outline of a long, thin face with an aquiline nose and just the hint of a tired eye. Laura didn't respond, so the man spoke again.

"*Forgive me for intruding on your thoughts. But I recognized the words and felt glad to hear them. He wrote once to me, too.*"

"*To you!*"

"*Does that surprise you?*"

"*I suppose nothing should surprise me any longer. But how could he have known about you or anyone from times to come?*"

The man chuckled—it sounded at once friendly and hollow.

"*He knew much. I, too, should have taken his advice. Though, to speak truly, I must say he knew more of the past than of the future, more of the past than even of his own time. That proves true for many of us who read and learn and write. You write as well, I suspect.*"

"*Oh, nothing to speak of,* Laura replied, *nothing that most people would know: I am no poet. I do scholarly work: articles, notes, a couple books on literature.*"

"*Ah, I see: a student—no, a scholar and a teacher! Your youth belies you. But I mean that as a compliment, not an insult.*"

No, don't worry: I will not trouble you. I speak only to tell you that what you're looking for you won't find here. This is my city, not his."

"Brother, how could you know what I'm looking for? We haven't met."

"Little Brother, *you would more accurately say. You must visit Arezzo, you know—you haven't yet gone there, correct? I'm sure you know he, Petrarca, was born there. You may find something . . . Young lady, please do an old man a small favor: tomorrow morning visit the Casa di Dante. You know where it is? Of course you do. You will find something there waiting for you that will surprise and I hope delight you. Ah, look at the boat coming down along the river: late to be out rowing, but look how quickly they fly along the water!"*

Laura looked west, and indeed a four-man scull was coming toward the bridge with surprising speed.

Night was falling rapidly. *"What do you suppose they're doing, practicing for a race?"*

Laura turned to look at the man, but he had gone.

She looked around and could find no trace of him.

She walked back and forth from one end of the bridge to the other, even looked in at the shops, but she could find no Franciscan monk, either brother or father.

Casa di Dante: she had of course visited it before as she had visited the tomb in Ravenna, but she wouldn't have thought to find anything new there. She could walk to it in a few minutes in the morning. Why should she do what the Franciscan suggested? He didn't even stay to explain. Yet why not do it? She hadn't visited the home in a few years and might enjoy going through it again. That would hardly take much time away for her research, and where had the research led her so far but to nothing?—almost nothing, except for a ghostly friar on the Ponte Vecchio on a beautiful May evening.

***

In the morning, after yogurt, rolls, fruit, and coffee, Laura took a pleasant walk into the center of the city to an angled, dun-colored building at a little corner of the Via Santa Margherita with its bust of the poet on the wall beneath a red banner identifying the museum. The museum houses a number of significant documents and some artistic reproductions, but Laura couldn't guess why the friar would ask her to come to a Dante museum for information related to Petrarch. She got there at a quarter after ten: the museum had opened at ten and was already seeing some traffic. She stood inside the door for a few minutes waiting to see if the man would appear. After a few minutes she spoke to a clerk, addressing her in Italian.

"*Excuse me, signora: have you seen a Franciscan friar here this morning?*"

"*No, I'm sorry. Are you looking for someone? Do you know his name?*"

"*It must sound odd, but no, I don't know his name. He asked me last evening to meet him here this morning: he was to have advised me on some research I'm doing on Petrarch.*"
"*Petrarch? Then why would he send you here?*"

"*I have no idea.*"

"*Then you have a mystery to solve. Perhaps you can help me solve one as well.*"

"*I'd love to.*"

"*You don't happen to be Professor Laura Campanelli?*"

"*Yes, I do.*"

"*Alora, then you have solved my mystery. Maybe this letter will help solve yours.*"

The woman gave Laura a wax-sealed envelope that had been sitting on the front desk. The front had her name penned in elaborate letters, fancifully medieval but readable.

"*Where did it come from?*" Laura asked.

"*I have no idea,*" the woman answered. "*It was here when I arrived this morning, and I was the one who unlocked the door. Could someone have left if for you last night?*"

"*I don't think so. I didn't see the man who asked me to come here until after you'd closed. I don't know how he could have left it before we met.*"

"*Then we still have a mystery. But you can solve part of it by opening your letter. I wish you a happy adventure!*" The clerk left to welcome a couple who had just come in.

Laura looked over the letter for a bit, then strolled southeast until she came to Santa Croce. She sat on the steps not far from the large statue of Dante—a tribute too late for their poet—and opened the letter.

Cara Professoressa Campanelli—I am very glad we met last night. I hope you will pardon what may seem to you my round-about way of trying to help. If you will go to the Biblioteca Nazionale Centrale—it is just a short walk from the statue outside Santa Croce—and ask for Signora Fratelli, she will have useful information: she has done what you call scholarship on Petrarch, and she will give you someone to contact in Arezzo. There if anywhere in Firenze you will find what you seek. I wish you nothing but the greatest and happiest success. With greatest respect, your friend and fellow writer . . .

The spelling was a little off, and the ghost of a signature—which looked like no more than initials anyway—had smudged so as to be unreadable, but she felt sure of its author. A letter from a ghost! How could he possibly have guessed that she'd walk, as she had, toward that church? A subconscious connection of one Dante site to another must have been a conscious and obvious connection to him. Anyone, despite his peculiarities, who had got a letter from Petrarch—or even claimed to—deserved some respect and attention from a scholar on quest.

The walk to the library brought some pleasant exercise, and another beautiful May day urged Laura to take her time even as question after question went through her mind. The Neoclassical library building on Pizza dei Cavalleggeri lost a great number of works when the Arno flooded in 1966, but it still has an enormous and prestigious collection. Laura met an officious-looking guard at the door, showed him her credentials, said she had been sent to see Signora Fratelli, and gave him her card for the librarian. He looked her over, nodded, and motioned for her to follow him in.

"Welcome, Professor Campanelli! We have your book on the modern descendants of Boccaccio—in Italian, of course." Signora Fratelli, with Laura's card in hand, spoke to her in only slightly accented English, and as much as she enjoyed conversing in Italian, she found the ease of using English an unexpected pleasure.

"So kind of you to mention it, Signora! But you're a scholar yourself: Petrarch, as I understand?"

"You know my work? Oh, that is extraordinary. I've published only a few notes in library journals and obscure records."

Laura felt guilty that she couldn't actually recall anything she read of the librarian's work, and she didn't want to embarrass Signora Fratelli or herself by saying too much about it.

Laura smiled broadly. "Everything we do helps—don't you think so? My last book got very little attention, but I still feel glad that I wrote it. Maybe it will help someone finish a dissertation sometime.

"I believe as you do. We can't all be Umberto Eco, writing book after book and novel after novel. Not that I'd even want to: that would leave me too little time for my family and friends. Please forgive me if I already think of you as a friend, but some passages in your first book made me feel as if I were talking to Boccaccio as well as to you. Forgive me if I haven't yet read the second, but we will order a copy for the library—what more can a writer ask of a librarian than that? But come in to my office and tell me why you've come all this way to talk to a librarian at the *Centrale*—it can't be just to ask about some notes in obscure journals, I suspect."

On the inside the Centrale hasn't the Renaissance beauty of some of the other great Italian libraries, but it has functionality and a great collection. Signora Fratelli took Laura upstairs to a small, neat office full of more books and papers than one would at first guess by its level of tidiness. Laura noticed an aroma of fresh coffee.

"We don't allow coffee among the books in the collection, but in my office here, amidst my own work, I permit myself a cup at this time of day to stimulate my thinking. Would you join me?"

"Thank, you, no: it smells wonderful, but I've been walking all morning."

"Ah, then let me pour you a glass of cold water instead."

"Wonderful. Signora, I received an extraordinary note this morning. May I tell you about it?"

"Certainly, Professoressa, but please call me Emma."

"Thank you, and I'm Laura. Maybe the best thing I can do is simply to show it to you." She handed the note from the Casa di Dante to the librarian. "Professor di Clemente from Cambridge got me interested in Petrarch's letters: he had a notion that a diligent detective may find more of the letters to Petrarch. I'm here looking for clues to those letters."

"Ah, that would be a rare discovery. And who wrote this note? The signature has smudged."

"Another strange link in the chain of events: I can't tell you. Let me say that better: I can't tell you because I don't know."

"But the writer has addressed it to you."

Laura explained about the ghostly Brother on the bridge.

"You do seem to attract mysteries—what fun! But I don't know what your ghost thought I can tell you. I can't imagine whom he thought I would know in Arezzo—unless he means Father Falcone: he and I have corresponded over some of the little notes we've published, and he knows much more about the little details of Petrarch's life than do I. As for the Father, I don't even know where he lives. I contact him by mail care of the Church of San Francesco. But he is not the parish priest there; I recall that he's a monastic, but I don't know where. I can promise nothing, only hope that he can help you more than I can."

"Do you have any idea how or through whom I can find him?"

Signora Fratelli thought for a moment, then smiled and picked up her office phone. She spoke quickly in Italian with what sounded to Laura like a Calabrese accent, but Laura understood most of it. The Signora concluded with a "thousand thanks," hung up the phone, and smiled again at Laura. "A stroke of luck: I have an old friend who's working temporarily as a clerk at the church. She knows Father Falcone—he comes there often—and he's due to visit tomorrow, filling in for the parish Priest for a special prayer service. If you can catch the train to Arezzo yet today, I suspect you can find the Father. Visit the church tomorrow morning and ask for Maria Giardino, my friend: she'll know what to do. I hope I'm not asking too much of you, to hurry off elsewhere when you're probably here to enjoy your time in Firenze—Florence."

"Not at all. *Mille grazie, Signora*—Emma. I'll just need to get back to my B&B for my bag."

"I'll check the train times for you before you go, and if you need to hurry, I'll get Eduardo, one of the guards, to drive you: he grew up here and knows the city streets as well as anyone."

"You've been so helpful," Laura said thankfully.

"My pleasure. Just one thing I'll ask in return: if you find anything interesting in Arezzo, stop back to tell me before you leave for home, or if you can't, send me a note care of the library. And if it's really interesting, maybe we can write something together."

"I can think of nothing I'd enjoy more."

In an hour Laura was on a train to Arezzo. Eduardo had driven her to her lodging and then down to the train station, and he had given her lots of useful information, including how to find the church, where to stay, and where to eat.

With only a brief stop at a little town called Incisa, the ride to Arezzo through a gently rolling landscape didn't take very long. Despite the season and the many small rivers and streams, the ground looked dry and dusty. Near Arezzo the valley opens a little wider, and the hills rise a little higher with fresher growth. The town even has a baseball team, which made Laura feel more at home.

From the train station she walked only a few minutes straight up the hill to the middle of town and checked in at the Hotel Vogue, which Eduardo had particularly recommended. While it looks unprepossessing from the outside and even in the lobby, she found beautiful, cool, comfortable rooms—named for painters, not numbered!— and Laura couldn't resist a bath and a nap before strolling out for supper. Having done so well with the choice of hotel, she wanted to try a family restaurant called Olga's that Eduardo had also recommended, but instead she walked up the hill to find the Church of San Francesco less than five minutes away. Too late to go in, she stopped instead at Terra di Piero, a wine and cheese shop, where she got a glass of Chianti Classico along with a salad and a beautiful cheese and fruit plate. She sat outside at a table on the square and listened as musicians played Italian music and people strolled in from all directions for dinner, gelato, or just music and companionship. She talked with an English couple who sat the table next to hers: they had come on a tour of central Italy for their fortieth wedding anniversary.

That night she went to bed early, and Laura awoke refreshed and ready to go. Early in the morning she walked up to see the Arezzo Cathedral, the tenth-century Santa Maria della Pieve, and the Basilica of San Domenico, with its famous Cimabue crucifix. She reached San Francesco at about ten o'clock. The bare, grey-brown façade, decorated only by lines of projecting stones, belies the treasures inside, including walls full of the beautiful Piero della Francesca *True Cross* fresco cycle.

Laura walked downstairs to the ticket office, where a youthful woman with a round face and enormous brown eyes greeted her. "*Benvenuto,*" the woman said, continuing in Italian. "*You wouldn't perhaps be Professoressa Campanelli?*"

"*Yes, good morning! Are you Signora Giardino?*"

"*Yes, oh, you've got here just in time! Father Falcone is upstairs waiting in the Bacci Chapel, but he's intending to stay only until 10:15. Come with me, please, and I'll introduce you.*"

Laura followed briskly as Maria Giardino led her up and into the main sanctuary, waving and nodding at the ticket clerk as they passed, and directly to the front of the chapel. "*Father Falcone is a Franciscan from the Eremo Le Celle monastery in Cortona. He comes here when the priests need extra help or sometimes just to visit the frescoes, and he practically haunts the Petrarch home at Arquà.*"

"*I understand he has an interest in Petrarch scholarship.*"

"*He does. Don't feel surprised if he tests you on it.*"

"*He may find my knowledge wanting. I know Boccaccio better, though I love Petrarch, too.*"

"*How could Laura not love Petrarch? There is Father Falcone. We'll stand beside him, and when he turns, I'll introduce you—best not to interrupt when he's concentrating.*"

The women waited for perhaps two minutes as Father Falcone stood still as a sculpture looking up at the section on Constantine's Dream. He turned partially around, glancing at Laura from the corner of his eye, and he addressed her directly in English in a deep, rumbling bass without any introduction.

"What do you think of Piero's faces, Professoressa? Of how he painted them?" He spoke in English with a Sicilian accent.

Laura waited for a moment before speaking, wondering how candid she should be with someone who knew the artwork intimately. She decided, as she normally did, that directness works best. The priest turned back toward the fresco as she spoke.

"They always seem to me to look inward rather than outward. Each face has its individuality, its own human beauty, but they don't look at each other or one another. They meditate rather than communicate."

Father Falcone's laugh was neither friendly nor punitive, but the nod suggested understanding if not complete agreement.

"For faces that engage one another, we must go to the next generation," he said.

"Luca Signorelli," Laura replied.

"You like Luca?" the priest asked familiarly.

"I do. I like Piero of course, but I have a special affection for Luca Signorelli. His images and his colors have force and vitality."

The priest inclined his head, as if to agree. "I'm glad you say so. My grandfather, my mother's father, claimed that their family descended from him."

"But your father's family are Sicilian," Laura added.

Laura looked at Emma Giardino, who smiled and winked, nodded to the priest, and left them to talk.

The priest remained silent for a long moment, looking up at the fresco. Then he spoke these lines:

> Et poi che 'l fren per forza a sé raccoglie,
> i' mi rimango in signoria di lui,
> che mal mio grado a morte mi trasporta . . .

Laura searched her memory, and to her surprise she found the next lines and spoke them in reply:

> sol per venir al lauro onde si coglie
> acerbo frutto, che le piaghe altrui
> gustando afflige piú che non conforta.

"From the sixth poem in the *Canzoniere*, I think? The concluding sestet," Laura said.

"Indeed, you are a scholar," Father Falcone said, turning his face directly on hers for the first time. You wanted to ask me something about Petrarca, the young Signora told me. You must know, though, that I am a priest first and only an amateur researcher."

"Yes, please: Signora Fratelli from the *Centrale* in Florence suggested I come to see you, and she thought Signora Giardino would know how I could find you."

"Ah, my dear Emma—we have published some work together, you know."

"I know of it, but I hope you will forgive me that I don't know it well."

"You should, and I'm sure that now you know more of it and its creators, you will come to know it well. What did you wish to ask?"

"I've done a very little work on Petrarch with Professor di Clemente from Cambridge. He got me interested in a pet project of his."

"Is he well, the old professor? I heard him lecture more than once at academic conferences, and we've spoken, though I doubt he would remember me."

"I'm sure he will remember, and I'll take him your greetings, but no, sadly, he's not in the best of health. Otherwise, I suspect he'd have come himself."

"So you are his assistant?"

"No. I should say rather his friend and junior colleague. Most of my scholarly work I've done on Boccaccio, but I've studied and written a little on Petrarch, too—and a bit on Dante, but then who hasn't?"

"Now that I think about it," Father Falcone said, "I imagine I can guess why you've come. I've heard buzz among the academics about some missing letters."

"That's it. The professor was hoping to find a lead on—"

"Letters to Cicero." The priest completed Laura's sentence."

"Yes, if more of them ever existed. I don't know that he ever expected to get his hands on one, but I think he hopes still to learn if any more actually survived."

"When did you last attend mass?"

Laura didn't quibble with the priest's *non sequitur*. "Last week at Santa Maria dei Fiori, and this morning I heard part of the early mass San Domenico: I got there too late for the beginning. Bless me, Father, for I have sinned: I took time for some extra strawberries at breakfast."

Laura was beginning to like the priest's gruff chuckle.

"*Te absolve*," he said, and for penance you should come here tomorrow morning for prayers—unless you must leave right away?"

"No, I'm staying here in Arezzo for at least another day or two."

"Have you visited Arquà and the Biblioteca Nazionale Marciana in Venice?"

"Yes, on previous visits, but I have yet to find the prize."

"You think of it as a prize?"

"Poor choice of words. Not every Indiana Jones finds the Grail, but all look for something that fascinates us and that allows us to add some small bits to the sum of human knowledge."

"Yes. But never forget the limits of *human* knowledge."

"Yes, Father."

"Who is *Indiana Jones*?"

"American movie character."

"I see. Americans and their movies . . . You've come here from Florence?"

"I teach in the States, but every time I come to Italy, I begin in Florence."

"Now *there* I understand you. But you are wondering if I can help you in this quest for a lost letter of Petrarch."

"Yes."

"Not at all a small request."

"No."

"And you think I can do that because . . ."

"Signora Fratelli sent me to you, and I trust her."

"You are old friends?"

"We are new friends."

"And you trust her already?"

"I do. I'm a good judge of character."

"And do you trust me?"

"Not yet, but I'm leaning that way." Laura tried not to smile, but the corners of mouth turned up just a little.

The priest laughed aloud, long and deeply, so that a number of the people there to enjoy Piero's frescoes in quiet turned disapproving glances toward him.

"Good for you. I have to return to Cortona, so I have no more time today, but if you can enjoy the hospitality of Arezzo for one more day, I will give you the only lead I can think of. It may come to nothing, but it is all I can offer. I will ask you to meet me at ten o'clock tomorrow at a location that may surprise you: the Museo Archeologico on the south end of town. Nothing is too far away here, but do you know where I mean?"

"I think so. I haven't visited it yet."

"Then tomorrow we shall. Ten o'clock exactly?"

"Yes: thank you!"

"Have you chosen a place for your dinner tonight?"

"No, so I'll be glad for your advice."

"Try Olga's: authentic regional cuisine and very much a family atmosphere."

"The very place I'd thought to go: a guard at the *Centrale* recommended it. I think a member of his family works there."

"Be sure to mention that: the people here value their family connections."

That evening Laura did have her dinner at Olga's: a gnocchi Pomodoro, grilled vegetables, and a mixed green salad. Her waiter was Eduardo's cousin, Antonio, and he did his best to make her feel welcome and well cared for.

"What brings you to Arezzo, Signora?" he asked.

Laura explained as well and as briefly as she could.

"I have a feeling," Antonio said, smiling broadly, "that you will find what you are looking for. Don't ask me why! It is just a feeling. You will find that here, if you haven't noticed already, we trust our feelings!"

She had spent the afternoon at the National Museum of Medieval and Modern Art, and to walk off a lovely dinner she spent the evening strolling up the hilly streets and looking in at the various shops and gelato stands. The walking and the evening's wine made her feel sleepy.

Laura slept well that night, but she woke early. A breeze had kicked up, so she tied her hair back in a ponytail, and she put on her comfortable Finn shoes to prepare for plenty of walking. After attending an early prayer service at

San Francesco as she'd promised, Laura made the short walk down below the train station to the archeological museum.

The museum, on grounds that once housed a Roman amphitheater and later a monastery, maintains excellent collections of pottery, jewelry, coins, mosaics, tomb furnishings, and stone busts. But Laura saw no evidence of any manuscript collections. Since she'd got there well before her appointment with Father Falcone, she paid for admission and took her time looking around. She passed an open door to what looked like a combination office and laboratory and saw a nun sitting there leafing through a pile of parchment pages. Laura was about to slip away so as not to disturb her, but the woman turned around and smiled at her.

"*Buon giorno, Signorina,*" the nun said genially. She had the brightest blue eyes and the smoothest, softest-looking skin that Laura had ever seen on a human being.

"*Buon giorno, Suora,*" Laura replied.

The nun continued speaking in Italian. "*Have you an interest in old manuscripts?*"

"*Yes, I have.*"

"*You are a scholar, a professor?*"

"*I am. And you are a scholar and a Benedictine.*"

The woman smiled with brilliant white teeth. "*Yes, but in reverse order: a nun first, and then a scholar. You are perhaps the woman the brother told me I might expect?*"

"*I suspect so, but not a brother: Father Falcone.*"

"*Forgive me, but I have not met Father Falcone. A Franciscan brother said I should look out for you. I've dug up these manuscripts for you, but you arrived earlier than I expected, so I have not had the time to search them first. But, then, you may enjoy doing that yourself: one never knows what treasures may appear among a stack of old documents.*" She smiled again, and her eyes and teeth seemed almost to beam.

She couldn't possibly mean the man from the bridge in Florence, Laura thought.

"*Here, Professoressa, please sit down and feel welcome. I need to go down the hall for a moment to look for someone who may help you, if you'll excuse me. Enjoy your search!*" The woman got up spryly, nodded, almost bowed to Laura, and scurried out the door.

Laura sat down, picked up a pair of cotton gloves she found on the table and put them on, and began carefully going through the pages. She found herself immediately engrossed in swatches of Latin poetry, groups of Roman and Italian letters from notables and unknowns alike, and finally what looked to be a manuscript copy of pages from Petrarch's *Africa*, perhaps even in his own hand. She felt the blood rise to her cheeks: if the manuscript were genuine, it was a treasure indeed. She had no sense of time passing until she recognized a deep, growling chuckle coming from behind her. There stood Father Falcone at the door.

"You've got here early and started before me," he said.

Laura stood to greet him. "Please join me, Father. I believe you'll be as astonished as I am to find these parchments unless you knew already what to expect."

"I knew they have some Roman manuscripts and perhaps a few of Petrarch's, but I did not know what to expect. What a perfect spot to search: this combination of modern Italy and ancient Rome . . . I guessed them worth your time, since you're in Arezzo already. You've found something interesting then? You'd better turn pages for me, since I brought no gloves, and I don't see another pair on the table."

"Did you speak with the nun? She was sitting here when I passed by and asked me to come in. I wasn't planning to scoop you."

"*Scoop*, yes, I know the term. All's fair in prayer and scholarship. What nun?"

"Sister . . . I don't know her name. I'm embarrassed that I didn't ask. She said she was expecting me, so I assumed that you had spoken with her and that she left to greet you and bring you here. But that may have been some time ago: I've been poring over these ever since."

"I can see why," Father Falcone said, looking intently as Laura turned pages for him. "It's just ten o'clock now, and I saw no nun—just happened to chance by the door, as apparently did you."

"Maybe she did mean the Franciscan on the bridge," Laura said, thinking aloud.

"What Franciscan on the bridge?"

"I'll tell you about him later. I seem to be getting series of clues on this trip from sources both human and divine."

Father Falcone, using cloth from sleeve to cover his fingers, had already begun leafing more rapidly through the pages so that he barely heard what Laura had said. "Ah! I don't believe this myself, and I have never suffered from a lack of belief."

Laura began to read. The hand was not easy to follow, but she could make out most of the words. "Renaissance parchment, I think, and a Renaissance hand. I dare say it looks like—"

"Petrarch's own. I've seen some of his writing, and if I am any judge, this looks just like it. And as you say, the paper is right, too—that's what drew me to it."

Laura scrambled for a second chair for the Father, and the two scholars began going through the document word by word, line by line. Father Falcone pulled a notebook and pencil from his pocket, and together they transcribed and later translated the contents. Here is what they found.

As I reread your letters, O Marcus Tullius, if I may be so bold to say so, I have studied your thoughts not only with my mind, but with my heart. Your advice has saved me, in my later years, more than once from trouble—if only Dante could have read your letters as I have. Now I better understand your perturbations—I had unfairly expected the coolest rationality when every man must now and again fall into emotional turmoil. I do not ask consistency—few men can keep to that—but for circumspection, which you better than anyone can understand. You will, I hope, forgive me the discourtesy, both to you and to myself, of offering advice of my own. Were it to reach you and you to take it, it might change your time and therefore mine as well—we can hardly know what good or harm could come of that. I will take the risk: the poet, like the philosopher, must show courage in his convictions and mercy to his friends. You have known exile, but I would spare you death before your proper time: you yet have work to do! Though you have good reason to fear and distrust him, you must refrain from naming Marc Antonius an enemy of the Roman State. He and Octavian will reconcile, and even Octavian cannot save you then, and for Antony's friends even your murder will not suffice. Take courage and observe prudence, my friend! May faith from a later age preserve you! Written in Arquà in the year of Our Lord 1373 by your friend across the centuries, Fr. Petrarca.

"A forgery?" Laura asked.

"Perhaps," Father Falcone replied. "But I think not. We must begin the process of authentication. It may take many years."

"I take comfort that we've found it—well, found something."

"So do I. We must talk with the head curator. You do seem to have had an extraordinary level of assistance, both human and divine, on your quest. Now what about that nun you were telling me about?"

***

That evening Laura had supper with Maria Giardino at a corner café in one of the streets below San Francesco

Basilica—she had been surprised and pleased to find a note from her when she'd returned to her hotel. Emma had visited the States twice, and they discussed travels in the US and in Italy.

"*Will you get back to Florence before you leave for home? Then you must have dinner at a place called Latini's: a little family-style restaurant hidden in an alley a couple blocks up from the Arno. I'll email you a map so you can find it.*"

After supper they walked up to Terra di Piero, got a glass of wine, and settled into a table outside to listen to some musicians playing in the piazza. Antonio from Olga's walked by, and they flagged him down to join them for a drink. Antonio and Maria told Laura all they could think of about Arezzo past and present.

"*Did you find what you were seeking in Arezzo, Professoressa?*" Antonio asked.

"*I think I did.*"

"*I have a feeling you have one more thing to find yet before you go home.*"

"*What's that?*"

"*I have no idea. I have only a feeling, not prescient knowledge. But as I've told you, I trust my feelings.*"

"*Stop by the basilica to see me in the morning before you go?*" Maria asked.

"*I will,*" Laura said. "*Thank you. I'll be leaving on the ten o'clock train, but I should have time to say good-bye.*"

In the morning Laura checked out of the Hotel Vogue very happy with her stay. She took the walk, less than five minutes, once more to San Francesco. When she got there,

Maria was waiting for her on the steps waving an envelope. Laura bound up the steps in two hops.

"Good-day, Laura! You have some of the leopard's gracefulness! Antonio was right: when I got here this morning, I saw a piece of parchment paper rolled up like a scroll with a second scroll rolled more tightly inside it, and someone had stuck it in a chink in the façade of the church. Look: I'll show you the spot— right here! You wouldn't even notice the hole from a distance, but up close you can see that you could fold a paper and place it in nicely. I just happened to see the edge of it sticking out from the wall. I thought it was a piece of litter, but then I read your name on the front. Imagine that! I did not look inside—maybe it's a love letter from Antonio! I won't pry. Or maybe it's a note from another of your ghosts."

They kissed each other on the cheek, and Laura promised to stay in touch. She put the involuted scrolls in the top of her travel bag and walked down to the train station, where she caught the on-time train back to Florence.

She found a comfortable seat on the train and tried to resist reading the mysterious letter, thinking she would keep it safer by opening it in her hotel room once she'd got to Florence. But curiosity got the better of her, and she unzipped her bag, pulled it out, and began to read the top page:

> *Dear Professoressa, I found something among the Petrarca papers at the Museo that you neglected to take with you. The curator gave me some trouble about it, but I*

won him over with the argument that since it is addressed to you, as you will see, it must be yours, and we should get it to you before you left Florence. I took the liberty of installing it at the Basilica San Francesco: I had a feeling you would visit there again, and as you've noticed by now, we Italians trust our feelings. I am truly happy that you found the letter you were seeking and as happy that you and the Father will bring knowledge of it to the world while leaving it still in its proper resting place here at the Museo. May God bless your work, your travels, and your life.—Sister Bernard

How extraordinary, Laura thought. She had begun to think the mysterious sister a ghost, yet the letter felt real. But then again, it appeared on Italian Renaissance parchment, hardly an easy thing to get now, and the writing, which took her some time to decipher, looked antique rather than contemporary.

Her heart began to beat rapidly as she gently opened the inside scroll—it felt as if it would crumble it if she failed to take care, but it had survived getting stuffed in the wall of the church and getting buffeted by wind, hands, and time. She read the first line, *My dearest Laura*, and almost fainted where she sat. She had just time to read it before the train arrived in Florence.

You will think perhaps that I have written this letter to the beloved Laura of my own time, but as I wrote backward in time to my dear friend Cicero, so I write forward to my equally dear friend Professoressa Laura. I am glad that you found the other letter I wrote to Cicero—I assure you of its authenticity, though no doubt your scholars will quarrel over it. This letter I write not for them, but for you. You will meet many men and women who will admire you for your work—you can do so much more than a woman can in my unenlightened time—so I ask not so much that you make the most of your opportunities for their sake as that you enjoy them! Life flies by. Joys appear now and then, while sorrows come in flocks. And one more thing I ask, because I know that though you have a calm and logical mind, you also have a passionate heart, though you have tended to hide it. You know that I cannot write such a thing without some hypocrisy and sorrow of my own, so I hope you will do what I did not, and find a companion, a partner with whom to share and enjoy your life. I have no means to tell you who or when that may be. I ask only that you keep your heart open for it. With much affection, written at Arquà, year of our Lord 1374, Fr. Petrarca.

The scholar in me tells me that this letter can't be real, Laura thought, but my heart tells me to enjoy it, believe it or not! She hugged the letter gently to her heart.

In Florence Laura got lodging for the night downtown at a boutique hotel just north of the Arno. She opened a window, stretched out on the bed in her room, and tried not to think about the letter: it had gained a hold on her, and she hoped a nap would ease the tension that tightened the muscles around her temples. But she couldn't sleep, so she wrote a note to Emma Fratelli and asked the proprietor to post it for her. She went out to attend an evening prayer service at Santa Croce and then followed Maria's map to Latini's.

The sort of place Americans might call "hole-in-the-wall," Latini's lies tucked away in an alley, the sort of place locals go to all the time and tourists find if they're lucky enough to get a tip. By the time Laura got there, a line had formed from the door nearly all the way to the end of the alley. But Maria had spoken so highly of it that she waited anyway—she hoped her last dinner in Florence would provide something special to conclude an adventure beyond a scholar's dreams. By the time she got to the door, the place looked full to bursting. The host held up a hand to request that she stop, and he seemed to be examining her face carefully.

"*Prenotazion?*" he said.

"*No, 'scuzi.*" Laura explained that it was her last night in Florence and she had come at the recommendation of a friend from Arezzo.

"Americana?"

"*Si, Signore.*"

The man put his hands on his hips, shook his head, and sighed.

"We make room for one more," he said, and he waved her in. She passed by with thanks, and then he held up his hand again in the "stop" sign—Laura heard a collective sigh from the people in line behind her.

Inside a waiter waved diners this way and that as they filled up tables family style. He looked at Laura, tilted his head, and waved for her to follow: "*Andiamo.*" Every chair at every table has already filled, Laura thought, but he led her to another room where a single seat remained at a table too small for the five diners already sitting there. Laura greeted the others both in Italian and in English, and they all gave a hurried but friendly greeting in reply—everyone looked nervous stuffed in with persons they had never met before and of whom they neither knew nor dared guess anything.

Another waiter quickly brought bread and an enormous jug of local wine. He came back soon to take orders, which didn't take very long, as the menu had only six options, which changed daily. After they had all made their requests, he welcomed then to Latini's and sped off to another table and then to the kitchen.

Some of the diners were speaking together—there were two couples and two single men, one who looked like he might be Scandinavian and another, sitting across from him, who looked Greek. As she was looking at the Greek man's features, she realized he was looking intently back at her. She was about to apologize for staring when he spoke to her in English.

"Laura? Laura Campanelli? Surely it can't be you."

"Yes. Do we know each other?" She looked more closely, and the man began to look familiar indeed.

"That makes me sad, that you don't remember me. But then I may not look the same after so many years. You look just the same, only taller." He smiled broadly, showing gleaming white teeth, and small wrinkles formed around his wide brown eyes.

"It can't be, not after all these years. We were children. Charlie, Charlie Michelakos?"

"Ah, you do remember. Have I changed so much?"

"Well, we were, what, ten years old when we last saw each other?"

"Must have been ten or eleven. We lived at the other end of the street from you, and then my father moved us to the other side of town to a bigger house, and then finally we went up to the City where he got a better job. But I would have recognized you anywhere. Are you here by yourself? Yes, so am I."

"Would you too like to sit across from each other so you can talk more easily?" The Scandinavian stood, bowed regally, and offered Laura his chair.

"I hate to trouble you, but, oh, thank you very much, that would be lovely. What brings you to Florence?" Laura asked, sitting opposite to Charlie.

"Business: I do some international accounting, and I have a number of clients in Italy and Greece. All those years of Greek school paid off."

"And you've learned Italian, too."

"The French we did in high school stuck for some reason, and I took three years of Italian in undergrad. But what brings you here?"

"I had some research to do here. Scholarly work. I'm a professor of Continental literature specializing in Italian."

"That doesn't surprise me. You were always the smartest one in our class. You've traveled a lot in Italy? Have you gone to Greece yet?"

"No."

"Oh, you should: you'd love it, especially the islands. Do you speak any Greek?"

"No, I studied ancient Greek in school, but never learned the modern. I can quote Homer for you, if you'd like." Laura smiled.

"I believe you!" Charlie said. "Please tell me about your work, Greek or otherwise. You have something in your face that shows me you've just made a great discovery."

"Something pretty obscure: are you sure you want to hear about it? A letter: a letter from Petrarch to Cicero."

"A letter! Didn't Petrarch live something like 1400 years after Cicero?"

"Yes. Isn't that something?"

"It certainly is. Tell me all about it!"

A WALK IN THE DARK

Epilogue

After the pageant in Act Four, scene 1, of The Tempest, Prospero
reassures his young audience so:

Our revels now are ended. These our actors,
As I foretold you, were all spirits and
Are melted into air, into thin air:
And, like the baseless fabric of this vision,
The cloud-capp'd towers, the gorgeous palaces,
The solemn temples, the great globe itself,
Yea, all which it inherit, shall dissolve
And, like this insubstantial pageant faded,
Leave not a rack behind. We are such stuff
As dreams are made on, and our little life
Is rounded with a sleep.

We may believe along with e.e. cummings that life is not a paragraph and death no parenthesis, and so the spirits in our stories flee beyond sleep to something better than a dream. Stories shared help make the interim, we hope, more than a pastime: a gift to live and enjoy.